RENO'S RENEGADES

Clint Reno lost all zest for living after his wife was murdered by marauding Comanches, and he drifted aimlessly, until hired guns tried to kill him. Three times they tried, but Reno saw to them all. The last bushwhacker died hard, gasping the name of the man who hired him. Reno rounded up his old wartime outfit 'Reno's Renegades', and in Mexico they encountered some of the bloodiest fighting Reno had known – but at the end he discovered the man who had sent the Comanches to kill his wife.

RENO'S RENEGADES

RENO'S RENEGADES

by

Tyler Hatch

Dales Large Print Books
Long Preston, North Yorkshire,
BD23 4ND, England.

British Library Cataloguing in Publication Data.

Hatch, Tyler
    Reno's renegades.

    A catalogue record of this book is
    available from the British Library

    ISBN 1-84262-351-6 pbk

First published in Great Britain 2004 by Robert Hale Limited

Copyright © Tyler Hatch 2004

Cover illustration © Faba by arrangement with
Norma Editorial S.A.

Published in Large Print 2005 by arrangement with
Robert Hale Ltd.

Dales Large Print is an imprint of Library Magna Books Ltd.

Printed and bound in Great Britain by
T.J. (International) Ltd., Cornwall, PL28 8RW

CHAPTER 1

HEAD SHOT

The bullet knocked Clint Reno out of the saddle, flailing back over the prancing horse's rump to sprawl on the dusty trail.

The second bullet kicked dirt into his mouth and, head ringing, blood beginning to crawl down his face, he instinctively rolled towards the trail's edge into some low brush. The ambusher raked the area and Reno crawled in behind a group of small rocks, lead ricocheting with angry buzzes and whines.

By then he had his six gun out and his hand was shaking as he blinked his eyes in an effort to clear his vision. Smoke drifted from the high rim of the pass and there was a flash as sunlight streaked along gun metal. Reno knew his six gun was next to useless at this range but he slammed three fast shots anyway, spun to his left, pivoting on his hips, looking for the horse. The dumb critter was standing with head up in the centre of the narrow trail, ready to run but not yet making a move. The killer read Reno's mind and sent two hammering shots between the horse's forefeet, sending it plunging away back through the pass, taking Reno's rifle out of reach. *The son of a bitch was playing with him!*

The cowboy swore, head buzzing and beginning to throb. He hugged the rock, the man on the rim holding his fire now – maybe reloading. Clint Reno used the time to punch out the used shells and replace them in the Colt's cylinder with fresh loads from his cartridge belt.

Still the man up there didn't fire again. Reno knew he had to use this time to find better shelter. It was risky but all he could do. He lifted his body over the low rock and hurled himself on to three yards of cleared ground, rolling and spinning desperately towards a higher boulder, its base dotted with small protective rocks.

He made it an instant before the rifle raked the shelter in a seemingly unending burst. The man must have emptied his magazine. *Getting desperate* – but why? It was lonely out here, where he had been scouting for water way ahead of the herd. The killer still controlled the situation. What had goosed him into wasting ammunition…?

Moments later Reno had the answer. A distant yell, a muffled clatter of hoofs, a ragged volley followed by random puffs and spurts along the rim as hastily-aimed shots chipped away at the granite.

He put two of his own bullets up there but there was no reply this time. Only the whinny of a horse high above followed by retreating hoofbeats.

The killer was lighting a shuck and in a damned hurry, too.

Reno slumped, the headwound starting to get to him now. His brain felt too big for his skull. The world began to reel and tilt out of plumb. The sky darkened. He clawed his fingers into the dust, trying to keep from tumbling off the planet, and as he started to slide away into the descending darkness, he heard a vaguely familiar voice call,

'There he is! In them rocks…! Hell, he's been headshot!'

It sounded like Hairy Jack Gage.

Good, he thought as the lights went out. *Go-oo-dd…*

Doc Charles in Henderson told him he was mighty lucky.

'An inch to the left and they'd be thinking

9

what to put on your headstone, young man.'

Reno, head swathed in bandages, was propped up in the iron-framed infirmary bed with pillows in striped cases. As always when he was in an infirmary as a patient – and there had been more than a few times over the years, four at least during the War – Reno was uncomfortable both physically and mentally. His skull thudded endlessly and he tended to see things in double vision. He was also nauseous.

'Concussion,' Doc told him. 'Mild enough, and it ought to clear in a day or two. That's why I'm keeping you here till I'm satisfied your condition is sound.'

'Hell, doc, I'll be all right – I was born in a saddle.'

Charles sighed. 'Why is it all you rannies who claim that not inconsiderable feat are so stupid? Is it because you all fall on your heads...? Look, son, someone tried to kill you and you told the sheriff you don't know why–'

'I don't.'

'I believe you. But count your blessings, man! You're here because of good luck and good luck only. If your friends hadn't come looking for you to tell you an Indian who had ridden into camp had led your herd to water, you'd be fertilizing the chaparral beside the trail through Honeytree Pass. Instead, in a day or so, you'll be able to ride out and catch up with the herd and get on with your life. Be grateful, son. Don't push your luck.'

Reno knew the sawbones was right and after he conned the man into allowing him to have his tobacco sack and papers, he settled down to wait for this concussion thing to clear up.

The shy young girl who assisted the medico brought him his tobacco, adjusted the pillows and bed covers, asked if he wanted fresh water in the bedside carafe in a barely audible voice.

'I'm fine, Carrie. Maybe you could pull down the blind on that there window, though – sun's a mite bright for my eyes…'

When she had gone, he rolled and lit a cigarette and had almost finished it when Tag Carmody, the trail boss, clumped in and gruffly handed him a grease-stained paper bag.

'Cookie sent in a fruit pie for you – you all right?' Without giving Reno a chance to say anything, Carmody went right on: 'Look OK, and Doc says tomorrow or next day you can ride out – likely so, leastways. Any ideas who the son of a bitch was?'

Reno started to shake his head but previously he had learnt that hurt too much. 'No idea at all, Tag. Guess I've got enemies but none I can think of would want to kill me. Did any of the boys see him riding out?'

'Hairy did, but it was just a glimpse. Said the horse was a dun, feller looked to be average height and he thinks he had a beard. Black – not much in that.'

Reno agreed and Carmody told him some details about the condition of the herd and how many miles they were making a day, where the helpful Indian had told them the next water was. It was obvious from his fidgeting that he was anxious to get back to his herd so Reno feigned tiredness (though it was only partly feigned) and Tag Carmody clumped out, saying he hoped to see Reno riding in in a couple of days.

He had hurt his back when he had taken the tumble from his horse and couldn't get comfortable in the bed. He mentioned it to Doc and he said he would have Carrie move him but she didn't turn up by dark. So while Doc Charles was at supper he moved himself – and was mighty glad to fall into the other bed two more along from the original. It had a better mattress and he somehow fluked the pillow arrangement so that he took the pressure off the sore part of his back.

Doc was annoyed at him, and swore because Carrie hadn't turned up, but grumpily allowed it was a sign he was recovering.

'Can I go tomorrow then?'

'Wait and see.'

'Aw, come on, doc, I can't...'

'Wait and see.' He hesitated, then said, 'Carrie's a good girl, but she works the saloons part time, has an invalid mother to care for and the damned old woman takes advantage of her good nature. I give her what leeway I can, because she needs the money. I'm telling you because I believe you're not stuffy enough to let such a thing bother you – don't prove me wrong.'

Doc left, blowing out the lamps, pulling the blind again, closing the door after him.

Reno tried to sleep but was determined not to ask for a draught: he didn't like being in control of any drug, which was one reason he rarely got drunk with the other cowhands at trail's end. Maybe a hangover from the War when, working undercover, he couldn't afford to have his senses dulled by booze – even if he acted as if they were on occasions that suited his assignment.

He was just dozing off when something

13

brought him back to full wakefulness.

There was a noise at the window and he saw a man's crouching silhouette. Then there was the sound of breaking glass and the thunder of two fast shotgun blasts. The bed he had vacated earlier erupted into showers of mattress stuffing and torn, flying pillows. Buckshot skittered about the room, pinging against glassware and metal objects.

Reno was on the floor on the opposite side of the bed before he realized he had moved. The gun he had slipped beneath his pillows was in his hand and he triggered two shots at the wrecked window. Wood splintered and a man grunted, then the shape was gone and the third shot slammed away into the night, thudding harmlessly into the framework of the building next door, a freighters' warehouse.

Ears still ringing, Reno heard the killer running away.

He thought to go after him, but stumbled across the bed between his and the one torn apart by the shotgun blasts.

Then the room seemed to be full of people – Doc, harassed and awkward in his nightshirt, trying to gain some control. The sheriff arrived and helped clear the rubbernuckers, then turned to the medic.

'Gotta talk with him, Doc.'

'After I finish my examination. Wait in the other room.'

'I'll wait here,' the lawman said, hefting his rifle. His voice was gravelly and Reno figured the man had been asleep and had to wake up in a hurry to see what all the shooting was about.

But he couldn't tell the sheriff any more than when Hairy Jack had first brought him into town. 'I just dunno why anyone would want to kill me, Sheriff.'

'You damn drifters – you make enemies all along your backtrails, bring trouble into my town, then make out you're a damn angel.' The lawman, a hard-faced, rawboned man in his fifties, stabbed a gnarled finger at Reno. 'You get outta Henderson tomorrow. Noon's your deadline.'

'I don't know if that'll be possible, Sheriff...'

'Doc – I want him outta my town by noon. I don't care if he's on his feet, in a saddle or in a pine box, but he better not be here one minute past noon.'

The man left angrily and Doc Charles shook his head.

'Got a peptic ulcer and a nagging wife. You'll have to excuse him.'

15

'To hell with him,' growled Reno. 'He don't care that I nearly got killed.'

'You'd better move into the main part of my house for the rest of the night. I'll see if I can find Carrie to come help with the move.'

When the girl did come, he hardly recognized her. She wore lip rouge and mascara, her bright red hair was piled on top of her head and there was a plunging neckline in her worn but clean dress. She smelled of saloon and was embarrassed, refusing to meet his gaze as she gathered clean sheets and pillows to take into the bedroom allotted to Reno in Doc's house.

'You must've heard about what happened, Carrie.'

She nodded. 'It – it's terrible. I'm – sorry, Mr Reno.'

'Why?' He frowned at the tremor in her voice.

She stepped back, clasping the folded sheets to her, eyes wide. He frowned. *He had somehow spooked her.* Then it hit him. She was apologizing, not because of what had happened but – *because she felt somehow responsible!*

Now how could that be–?

He put out a hand suddenly as she went to leave and she turned back, eyes filling now.

He spoke quietly. 'Did someone ask you which bed I was using in here, Carrie?'

She started to shake her head quickly, but then her teeth tugged at her lower lip and she began to cry.

'It's all right, Carrie,' he said gently. 'You weren't to know. Just tell me what he looked like.'

It took a little time but he learned that the man was about average height, had a black beard and a broken nose with a slit in one nostril, likely an old knife wound. And he was generous with his money.

'I thought he was a friend of yours. He mentioned paying you a visit,' she wailed, using the fresh sheets to dab at her eyes and wipe her moist nostrils.

'Well, he did that. You wouldn't know what kind of horse he was riding...?'

She gasped. 'I – I did look out of the window of the room we – used and saw him leading a light-coloured horse towards the livery. It – it was likely a dun...'

He smiled, patted her shoulder. 'Thanks, Carrie – lucky I moved beds without you knowing.'

He had a couple of dollars in his trousers and offered her one but she refused. 'OK. Tell Doc I've changed my mind – I'll sleep

17

here tonight. That man won't be back.'

When she had gone he got dressed, a little unsteady on his feet but gaining strength from the anger that was rising within him. There was a chance he might still catch up with this son of a bitch.

The man wouldn't run straight back to the livery after the shooting – it would be a guilty move and he could strike trouble from the night hostler or, at least, the man would most likely call the sheriff. He would be confident that no one had seen him and he would just hang around like an innocent until things calmed down enough for him to go get his horse and ride out casually.

The man was a professional: tenacious, mulishly determined to finish the job he had started out at Honeytree Pass.

Reno decided to go meet the killer face-to-face.

CHAPTER 2

TARGET

Reno had been up in the livery loft for an hour when the bearded man came in and, without waking the snoring hostler in his small cubicle of an office, made for the stall where the dun had been grained and curry-combed.

He was reaching under the horse's belly for the cinch-strap when Reno stepped into the stall, cocked sixgun in hand.

'Like a word with you pardner.'

The sound of Reno's voice had a dramatic effect on the bearded man. He was good – and fast. Without hesitation, likely recognizing Reno by the bandage around his head, he changed the direction of his hand under the dun's belly and punched it in the genital sheath. The animal whinnied and reared, pawing the air, and the killer heaved it backwards while it was on its hind legs.

Reno had to throw himself quickly aside to avoid being trampled, and the bearded man palmed up his Colt and fired, his lead kicking straw and muck against Reno's trousers, sending the already frantic horse into a series of bucks that splintered the stall partition and brought down hobbles and bridles and saddle gear. Reno rolled in the aisle, shooting across his belly as the man clambered over the far stall partition and dropped into the next box.

Reno leapt up and skidded around the corner, vaguely aware that the hostler was yelling. He saw the bearded man running for the rear doorway that led to the livery's corral section and he dropped to one knee, steadied his right hand with his left and thumbed off two shots.

The fleeing man was hurled forward as if kicked by a mule. He smashed face-first into a corral rail and slid off awkwardly, starting to go down. He clung to a rail with his free hand and his body twisted as he brought up his smoking gun and triggered at Reno.

Reno shot again and the man slammed back, bounced off the rails and spread out on his face in a pile of dung. The sheriff came pounding down the aisle before Reno had turned the man over and flicked some of the dung off his face. The lawman was mighty angry as Reno looked up.

'Dead.'

The sheriff grunted. 'Know him?'

'Never seen him before.'

'Makes no nevermind – your noon deadline's just been brought forward. I want you out of my town in one hour.'

'Doc might give you an argument.' Reno was feeling the strain, and wanted nothing more than to crash on to a bed and close his eyes.

'He can try, but if you're fit enough to have a running shoot-out with this *hombre*, you're fit enough to ride.' The rifle barrel rose to cover Reno. 'Unless you'd rather spend a few weeks in my jail while I look into this...? I believe it's your call, Reno.'

The next attempt was made two weeks later in a Colorado town at the southern end of the great San Louis Valley in Castillo County.

The herd had been driven to and sold in Socorro and after collecting his pay, Reno had drifted across to the valley for no special reason except he hadn't seen it before. His life had been kind of aimless for a long time now, but he didn't want to fight it because that would mean thinking about the reasons for his aimlessness – and that was one thing he didn't want to do.

21

The images were there constantly, behind his eyes, mixed in with the worst scenes of the War that he had witnessed. He didn't want to drag either thing to the level of consciousness and sometimes dreaded the night when the wild dreams claimed him.

But his head was almost healed now, only a small scar at his temple and the hair would grow over that soon enough. He wasn't really a gambler, but one night in a saloon in the valley town he sat in on a five-card stud and after initially losing most of his hard-earned wages, he hit a winning streak.

A two-hundred-dollar winning streak.

And two hundred bucks was mighty welcome. Of course there were moans and groans from the other players as his streak continued and he looked warily for anyone who seemed as if he might want to start hinting at bottom-card dealing. But the threat didn't come from the players. It came from one of the spectators who had gathered in a loose group to watch this rawhide cowboy pull in pot after pot, the stack of bills and silver coins in front of him growing in size noticeably.

A deep voice said casually, 'Was I playin', reckon I'd be watchin' the bottom of the deck mighty close.'

There was abrupt silence around the table although the usual night-time murmur of the saloon bar continued unabated. Reno flicked his gaze around the players, mostly locals, although one man claimed to have come down from Oregon. They all seemed genuinely startled so it wasn't likely the man who had made the remark knew any of the players.

Then Clint Reno half-hipped in his chair and slowly looked up. There was a man who seemed fresh in from the trail – Reno had been smelling smoke and wild vegetation for the last twenty minutes when he thought about it. The man was only medium size, his clothes needed to be cleaned, or brushed of loose leaves and dust at least, and he wore twin guns. He nursed a whiskey bottle in his left hand, and tugged innocently at one ear lobe with the fingers of his other hand. But his eyes met and held Reno's and they were brittle, penetrating, knowing – and most of all challenging.

'Why don't you sit in, friend?' Reno invited calmly. 'Right across from me where you can watch as I deal.'

The man smiled – at least his lips peeled back from smoke-stained teeth. He shook his head. 'Nah – I ain't got enough money to lose it that way. It'll disappear fast enough just spendin' it honestly.'

Now that was it, and everyone within earshot knew it. The card players scraped back their chairs and began to stand, moving out. The small crowd around the table made plenty of room.

Clint Reno laid down his cards and stood slowly, turning to face the gun-hung man who was taking a swig from the bottle now, his gaze watching Reno's every move.

'A loose mouth can get you into a heap of trouble, friend.'

'I ain't your friend, Reno.'

So, Reno's hunch was right: the man was on the prod. He wanted a gunfight. With *him*. And Reno's belly lurched as he realized this was yet another deliberate attempt on his life.

'I know you?' he asked, already knowing the answer. The man shook his head just a tad. 'I don't need to know you to recognize a four-flusher.'

Reno sighed. 'Then we better get this settled.'

That threw the gunman for an instant; obviously he hadn't expected Reno to be so ready to match gunspeed with him. Then he dropped the whiskey bottle and it smashed on the floor, but Reno didn't look down – he knew that old trick to distract the opponent. Instead his gun came up in his hand, blazing as the other man's Colts cleared leather.

Reno put two bullets into his chest and the man reeled back almost to the bar before tripping over his own feet and falling, one of his guns going off and driving a slug into the sawdusted floor. He jarred to his knees, swayed briefly, eyes wide, and then fell forward on his face.

Reno's smoking gun was already cocked as he looked around the silent crowd. No one was going to buy in, but he kept hold of his gun until the law arrived and then was told to holster the weapon or die where he stood.

Sheriff Magill was youngish, no-nonsense, ready to use the Greener he held with both hammers under his thumb. 'The man you just killed was known hereabouts as Slick Dawson and he didn't get the name because he used a lotta soap. Now who you be, mister?'

Reno told him his name and answered other questions about where he had been and what he was doing in town. Magill's face didn't give away any his thoughts.

'What was your beef with Dawson?'

'He bad-mouthed me when I was playing

cards. No reason. He was on the prod.'

Magill nodded. 'Slick was like that – but he was also a gun-for-hire. Any reason why he might've wanted to kill you – other than not likin' the way you played cards?'

Reno shook his head. The sheriff had just confirmed his suspicions: someone had put Dawson up to prodding him into a gunfight, apparently confident Dawson would out-gun Reno.

'I heard somethin' about you not long back,' the sheriff said, musing. 'Yeah – over to Henderson. You're the one shot it out with Ditch Sawtell, right?'

'I don't know any Sawtell, but a man tried to kill me twice while I was in Henderson and we shot it out in the livery.'

'Yeah, that's it – Sawtell was another gun-for-hire. Seems you ain't too popular, Reno.'

'Well, hell, Sheriff, I dunno what's going on! Far as I know I haven't riled anyone enough for them to hire *pistoleros* to kill me.'

'I'd say you were wrong there, pardner. Someone's out to get you – but you ain't gonna be got in my town. You collect your winnings and light a shuck. I'll see you to the edge of town.'

'You could let a man stay overnight!'

'I could but I ain't gonna. Now come on, Reno. If you need some persuadin'…'

The shotgun barrels lifted casually and Reno, mouth tight, nodded and turned to gather up his winnings.

He went to Alamosa and on to Del Norte on the northern reaches of the Rio Grande where he learnt that a winning streak didn't last forever.

Busted-broke, he swamped out the saloon for two days before getting a job with a mule-team freighter who aimed to cross the Sangre De Cristos and deliver supplies to the new goldfields at Pyramid and make his fortune. The mule-skinner was called Pug Solomon, a dirty, buckskin-clad type who stank worse than the animals he hazed around the south-west of Colorado. He had no teeth of his own, but kept a set of wooden ones he had carved and which he pushed into his mouth at mealtimes.

They didn't fit properly, protruding some so that his lips almost pursed, and made disgusting sucking, whistling noises when he chewed. Also much of the food spilled out into Pug's beard and for the first few days Reno wondered what in hell he was doing there. Pug Solomon turned his stomach when he ate, but for all his rough ways and foul-mouthed talk he was kind enough. Reno suspected he could be a soft-touch if approached just right.

'Don't say much, do you?' Solomon remarked around the campfire one night, the act of talking while eating spilling most of the boiled wildfowl egg into his beard. He cupped a hand, caught it and stuffed it back between the clacking teeth.

Reno looked up and quickly averted his gaze, then shook his head. 'My old man always taught me when you got nothing to say, say nothing.'

Pug thought that was a good one and roared with laughter, spraying food in Reno's direction. He brushed pieces off his shirt sleeve irritably.

'By God, Pug, the first thing you ought to do when you make your fortune selling these goods to the miners is buy yourself a proper set of teeth.'

Solomon blinked, took out the homemade gnashers, all caked with partly-masticated food, and held them up for inspection. 'What's wrong with these?'

'They're disgusting, that's what's wrong.' Reno stood abruptly. 'Sorry, Pug, can't watch you eat and I can smell you even upwind from you twenty yards away.'

'Aw, that's them damn mules, rubbin' agin my clothes. They stink like hell.'

'Try washing your clothes once in awhile. I'm quitting, Pug. Thanks for the job, but now I know why no one else would take it. *Adios.*'

Solomon didn't seem surprised he was quitting. 'Hell, I dunno, I've never managed to keep a man goin' over them mountains yet. Well, you got a few bucks comin' for the work you've already done. Can't pay you till I sell the stuff, though.'

'You're an honest man, Pug. See you some time.'

He rode out next morning, a friendly enough parting, and Solomon watched him go, hawked and spat and then began berating the string of mules which Reno had helped him load before leaving.

It took Pug four days to cross the Sangre De Cristos and he was surprised to be met by a deputation from the miners up at Pyramids. They had been expecting him and his goods were sold in their entirety on the spot.

In the town itself, the bars and whorehouses soon got back most of the money the population had spent on the stores, and Pug Solomon invested his last dollar in a bottle of sourmash brewed up by one of the more enterprising men whose claim had turned out to be utterly devoid of the rich yellow metal.

'Puma's piss, is what it is,' Solomon declared after two sips. But to make sure, he took several more and before long he was passed out down by the creek.

It was there that a man who looked nothing like a miner found him. He picked up the sleeping mule-skinner – afterwards carefully wiping off his leather gloves on the grass: and threw him into the creek. Pug came round, spluttering and half-drowned, blinking.

'Now what you go an' do that for?' he slurred.

The man, tall, rail-lean, skull-faced, waded out and grabbed Pug's greasy collar as the older man turned to plunge away. He dragged the mule-skinner back to the shallows, threw him face-down and planted his boot on the back of his head, grinding his face into the mud and gravel.

Pug had almost drowned before the man pulled him up and flung him against the bank. As the oldster burped and coughed up muddy water, the stranger placed a boot against his heaving chest and pinned him there. When he leaned forward he held an ivory-handled Colt which he waved in the frightened old man's face.

'Clint Reno.'

Pug Solomon blinked. 'Quit – t'other side of the Sangres…'

He screamed and writhed as the blade foresight of the gun ripped open his left cheek and then rapped him painfully across the bridge of his pug nose. Blood spilled from the nostrils.

'Where'd he go?'

'I – I dunno. He never said…' Pug screamed again as the gun barrel whipped back and forth, opening both cheeks now, ripping up one ear.

'Where – did – he – go?'

'I told you he never – *wait!* Aw, Christ, hold up a minute – I – I need a drink.'

The gun gestured to the muddy water. 'Help yourself – or I can hold you under while you drink the creek dry.'

Pug cowered and then two burly miners appeared, having been attracted by his screams.

'Hey! What the hell you doin' to him, you son of a bitch!'

'Yeah, leave him be you–'

The lean man's gun roared twice and Pug watched in horror as the miners were blown off their feet and rolled into the creek, their blood making red smoke in the muddy water. His eyes bulged. Killings on the fields were rife and he knew no one would bother about the dead men – there was no law up here and anyone sticky-beaking would take one look at this skull-faced bastard and turn tail immediately.

'You've had long enough to think about it,' the killer said and Pug held both hands in front of his face. It didn't save him. All it did was get him a mess of broke fingers and, almost crying with the pain he said,

'He mentioned Cañon City – was gonna try an' pick up a trail-herdin' job to Colorado Springs. He's a drifter. He don't make plans and stick to 'em...'

'Well, I do. And I plan to kill Clint Reno by the end of the month. I've set myself that goal.'

'What – what you gonna do with – me?'

'I'd kill you and leave you for the timber wolves, but I like wolves and you'd likely poison 'em.'

'I – I won't say nothin'!'

'Aw, I know that. I can guarantee you won't.'

The man smiled and it sent a gut-churning chill through Pug. He holstered his gun and drew the gleaming blade of an Arkansas toothpick from a sheath inside one of his high halfboots. Pug Solomon cringed as the man reached for his hair and said,

'Let's see that rotten tongue of yours, you stinkin' ol' varmint!'

CHAPTER 3

THE MAN

It was a small herd and only required three men to drive it from Cañon City to the railhead at Colorado Springs.

Reno had been hired as the top hand and the other two cowboys were brothers named Browning, Ed the elder, Jace the younger one. They knew cows well enough, but tended to go in for a lot of sky-larking and time was wasted chasing after strays because they hadn't been doing their job properly.

Reno told them about it and all Jace said was, 'What you gonna do? Fire us? Out here? Leave you to drive the herd yourself?'

'Take it easy, Jace,' Ed said quietly. 'We been playin' the fools an' Clint's right to take us to task. Sorry, Clint. Won't happen again.'

Reno nodded but Jace, hotheaded snapped, 'You don't speak for me, brother! I do my own talkin'-up.'

'You saying you're gonna keep on clowning about?' Reno asked and Jace's jaw jutted.

'If I want to, yeah. You ain't payin' us, Reno.'

'No, but the rancher is and he's entitled to get value for his dollar.'

'Aaah – you think you're still in the goddamn army. Hey, Reno? The War's been over for ten years, 'case you din' know.'

'Now that's enough,' Jace!' snapped Ed Browning, looking embarrassed at his brother's sass. 'You quit this an' we'll–'

'I don't like takin' orders from him! He come in after we got the job but Hanrahan made him top hand!'

'I worked for years to become a top hand, Jace,' Reno said quietly. 'Now you settle or I'll do it for you.'

'No need for that, Clint,' Ed said quickly, but Jace chose to take it as a challenge and rushed in at Reno, his big, knotted fists swinging.

But he was clumsy and let his anger get the best of him. Reno dodged the first barrage, easily fending off the wild blows, and clipped the kid smack-dab on the point of the jaw. Jace Browning dropped like a poled steer and Ed knelt by him quickly. When he looked up, the elder Browning's mouth was tight and he clenched his fists as he stood. Reno held up a hand.

'Don't do it, Ed. I can put you down just as easy as I did Jace. But while we've been trading insults, the damn herd's scattered. Now let's get the cows herded up again and we'll continue this if you want...'

Before they had finished rounding up the strayed cows Jace had come round and was rubbing his jaw gingerly. He shrugged off Ed's arm about his shoulder and, surly, refused to eat supper with Reno and Ed that night. He moved his bedroll several yards away, sulking.

'He'll come round by mornin'. Just feelin' the sap in his veins,' Ed told Reno as they sat by the fire, eating charred but palatable hunks of jackrabbit. Jace was sullenly chewing on some strips of jerky.

'Well, I don't much care whether he comes round or not, long as he does the job he's being paid for,' Reno replied. 'We'll make an early start tomorrow. Let's turn in.'

Ed washed up his eating gear and went to

his bedroll. The fire died down to coals and Jace, too, turned in, regretting spreading his blankets so far from the warmth of the fire but too stubborn to move them any closer.

That stubbornness cost him his life.

The skull-faced man came out of the darkness just before midnight, went to the bedroll set apart from the other two, thinking, naturally enough, that this would be the blankets of the man he had come to kill seeing as he was the one in charge. It's what *he* would do, sleeping apart from the hired hands, the killer figured.

The herd was quiet in a natural pen at the end of the draw and the horses were tied to a picket line strung between two trees. He figured he might as well kill them all anyway and fired two shots into the head of the sleeping figure he believed was that of Clint Reno.

He was unprepared for the reaction from one of the prone figures down the slope.

At the crash of the first shot Reno come rolling out of his blankets, Colt in hand, hammer going back under his thumb as he spun towards the sound, just as the killer fired his second shot into Jace Browning's head.

Reno didn't hesitate. He triggered and the dark figure was hurled back, doubled over, as the bullet took him in the stomach. Reno leapt over Ed Browning who was scrambling wildly out of his bedroll now, and ran to the killer. The man was holding one hand against his bleeding stomach and, face twisted in pain, started to lift his gun. Reno kicked it from his hand, swung the boot again and laid it alongside the skull-faced man's head. He fell unconscious and Reno knelt by Jace's bedroll, looking up at Ed, face showing pale in the dull light from the coals, and shook his head.

'Sonuver put two bullets into him.'

Ed let out an anguished cry and spun towards the downed gunman, then swung his gun up. Reno slammed his gun barrel across Ed's wrist and the man howled as his Colt dropped. He clutched his hand against his chest.

'Goddamnit, why'd you do that! Jace was my kid brother and he murdered him!'

'I aim to find out why,' Reno said and his tone was such that Ed didn't give him an argument.

Instead, he knelt beside Jace and took one look at the mess the man's head was in, crawled away and threw up. Reno had fetched his canteen and poured some water over the skull-faced man. He shook him roughly and the pain brought the man round. He flopped over on to his back and looked up at Reno with dulled eyes, clawing at his stomach wound.

'Finish – it, damn – you!' he gritted.

'Not yet. First you tell me who you are and why you killed that young cowboy.'

'Young...? Weren't that Reno?'

'I'm Reno. You came after me?'

The man didn't answer and Reno shook him again. He moaned, writhed. 'Don't...!'

'You came after me?' Reno repeated and the man nodded. 'Who are you?'

'They call me – "Death's Head".'

'Judas! He's a cold-blooded killer!' gasped Ed Browning. 'They say he'll kill anyone long as you pay him enough.'

'Hired assassin – who hired you to kill me?' No reply. Reno gripped the man's shoulder, pulled him half erect and slammed him back hard. The man screamed.

'Hey, Clint! Let *me* at him! He killed my brother an' one way or t'other he's gonna die if he don't talk, right?'

'Well, if he thinks he's gonna die easy he's a long way from being right.' Reno leaned towards Death's Head. 'You hear me? During the War when we were prisoners for a while, I saw a man gunshot. The Yankees wanted some information out of him. A sergeant put his boot heel into the wound and stood on it with all his weight. The Reb told him what he wanted to know within ten seconds.' Reno stood over the prone killer and lifted a boot above the man's stomach. 'Let's go for the record – anything less than nine seconds counts, OK?'

Death's Head screamed. 'Noooooo! Don't – aw, Jesus, it hurts!'

'Not as much as it will if you don't tell me who hired you.' Reno lowered his boot towards the man's midriff and Death's Head shouted,

'Colonel Skinner! Colonel Mason Skinner!'

Ed Browning was startled to see Reno literally jump backwards and freeze. He frowned and stared down at the moaning killer, his face pale.

'Hell's teeth!' Ed breathed. 'You know this Colonel Skinner?'

Slowly, Reno's head came around and the suddenly shock-dulled eyes looked back at Ed. Browning thought he wasn't going to answer, he was silent for so long. Then he said in a hoarse whisper,

'He's my father-in-law!'

The colonel's security hadn't improved,

Reno allowed to himself as he sprawled in the branches of the elm and slowly raked the field glasses over the grounds of the large estate with its pillared two-storied house on a slight rise. It was surrounded by gardens and shrubs and a few trees, also an area made private by head-high privet hedges.

Reno easily spotted the guards. Still the same amateur set-up – guards standing around in the one place, scattered sparsely around the grounds. Instead, the colonel should have broken up their area to watch into smaller portions and each man ought to patrol it constantly or, at least, on fixed or random tours. Likely there were no dogs, either. Another thing he would have insisted on if he had been in charge.

Still this was daytime; the routine might be different at night. The colonel had plenty of enemies and Reno assumed the chief bodyguard was still Stretch Kincaid, seeing as precautions were just the same as the last time he was here.

Hell! That was more than two years ago, closer to three...

So Reno climbed down from the tree, mounted the sorrel gelding he had hired in St Louis and went on back to town. After supper, he slept for a while down on the riverbank under an old boatshed, woke some time before midnight, then rode back to Colonel Mason Skinner's estate north of town at Bellefontain.

He climbed the same tree he had used that afternoon and while it was more difficult to see over the high stone walls with their barbed wire and broken glass set in cement on top, he made out the guards – the night shift, presumably, but still lounging in designated places, not patrolling the grounds where they might do some real good. Confidence, Reno allowed. *Or the colonel's orders. He'd always been stubborn.*

He had no trouble going over the wall. A big chestnut with unpruned spreading branches just tipped the barbed wire. It was a simple matter to shin out along an appropriate branch, swing his legs clear of the wire – they just might have it linked to tin cans somewhere that would clatter if the wire was touched – and then drop to the ground.

He almost came undone right away as a guard who had been dozing under the tree with his back against the trunk, grunted and started to come awake. Reno put him back to sleep with his gun butt. He kept the Colt in his hand as, crouched double, he made his way around the wall's perimeter not

41

worrying about standing on the gardens and their plants because the softer soil muffled his progress.

Near the side where he knew there was a railed patio and double glass doors that gave access to the Colonel's study, he left the wall's comforting shadow, ran across open ground to another garden of flowering shrubs, and trampled a couple before swinging over the stone railings.

'Judas priest! Who's that?' Another startled guard leapt up, and this one had a gun in his hand as he clumsily stepped out of the shadows and ran forward to meet the intruder. Reno sighed: *goddamn amateurs!* He stepped nimbly aside, cracked the man's gunhand with his Colt's barrel to get rid of the weapon and then slugged him hard as the man howled and bent over.

Reno went to ground in deep shadow, waiting to see if the guard's cry brought a response, but nothing happened. The blade of his hunting knife sprung the lock on the doors and he stepped inside into the lamplight, seeing the startled colonel at his large oak desk half-rising out of his chair, a pen in one hand, mouth sagging open.

'*You!* My God, they told me you were dead!'

'You're too tight with a dollar, Colonel, I told you that a long time ago. You get what you pay for and you paid for amateurs.' He gestured behind him as he pulled the curtains across the door. 'I could've killed them all in less than three minutes. As it is, two are going to have sore heads, and the rest seem to be sleeping.'

'By God, that better not be so or they'll be out of here on their butts so fast...' Skinner, a large man, fiftyish, running to fat with easy living now, steel-grey muttonchops bristling from his red face, broke off and slowly sat down, realizing his main problem was facing him – right here, right now.

'Still cooking the books?' Reno asked casually, gesturing to the account books and papers on the desk.

'You son of a bitch! How come you're not dead?'

'Not my time to go, I guess. Why the hell're you trying to have me killed?'

'Why the hell wouldn't I? You killed my only child!'

Reno was dead sober now, his rugged face tightening. 'I didn't kill her! It was the Indians and you know it.'

'You took her to that Godforsaken place! That wasn't bad enough, but you had to go

43

off rustling cattle down in Mexico – *left her alone, for Chrissakes!* Out there! In Comanche country! A woman who didn't know how to churn butter or even sew a button on a man's shirt, let alone how to fire a gun to protect herself!'

Reno sighed wearily. All this had been said before and he had run it through his mind every single night since Elanor's tragic death, no matter how hard he tried to suppress it beneath his consciousness. He was tied in knots inside right now, the rage that had brought him here swamped by this greater guilt that he had carried with him for three years...

'You never accepted that Elanor was afraid of you, did you, Colonel?'

'That's a lie, damn you! It was you who turned her against me! With your sly rebel ways and your lies... Why, you didn't even tell her your real name!'

Reno frowned. *That was a new one.* But he let the big man rant on. The colonel had to stand now, couldn't contain his anger sitting at his desk. He strode around the room and Reno turned slowly to watch him.

'I checked on you. Oh, it was too late and something I should've done a lot earlier, but I didn't really believe that Elanor would run away with you. Your name is Reynolds, Clinton Reynolds! And you were a lousy sergeant in that rabble army, not a lieutenant as you told her!'

'It *was* an army of rabble, Colonel. I'll give you that. Tough men fighting for their way of life, most of them uneducated. No one could even spell a simple name like Reynolds – "Ren" was about as far as they could get and one day, after months of it, one man added an "o" and I said that was good enough. "Reno" went down on my papers and I became Sergeant Clint Reno.'

Skinner grunted, feigning disinterest.

'But I was a sergeant only with my squad. I was chosen for secret work behind enemy lines in what they called the Ghost Troop. It was there I was promoted to lieutenant after a couple of successful sorties against you Yankees.'

The colonel's fat lips were squeezed into a pale, hateful line. 'You and your *Reno's Renegades!* A bunch of cut-throats and killers!'

'Well, none of us were playing kiss-and-tell, Colonel – but they were more than that. They were expert in their own fields: explosives, silent killing, break-and-enter, language. We raised hell with your columns and pay-trains and ambushes – but you know all that, just won't admit how much damage we caused.'

'You were killers! Sneaking, belly-dragging, lying killers!'

Reno was tired of this, and cut in abruptly. 'The War's over. Time you realized it Colonel. So why, after a couple of years, did you start sending assassins after me?'

Skinner suddenly smiled and Reno frowned – then realized he hadn't been watching closely enough. Skinner had yanked a cord or somehow signalled for help. And now the door burst open and Stretch Kincaid came charging in, cocked six gun in hand. He took one look at Reno who was coming out of his chair in a blur of speed and rage towards him, holding his fire.

Reno spun his chair into the man's path and Kincaid was good enough and fast enough to dodge it, and swung up his gun as the colonel screamed, 'Shoot him!'

Reno grabbed the man's arm and twisted savagely, Kincaid yelling as the gun fell. Reno pulled him in close and brought up his knee between the man's legs. Kincaid groaned sickly and fell writhing and then there was the flat crack of a derringer and somewhere behind Reno glass shattered. He saw Skinner setting the derringer's second barrel, and hurled himself bodily across the desk.

The gun went off and wood splintered, and then Reno's Colt's barrel opened a wound in the colonel's forehead. The man groaned and, dazed, blood sliding down his face, tried to get up. Reno stood, twisted a grip into the collar of the man's jacket and lifted him bodily, slamming him down so violently into the desk chair that the wood creaked and groaned with the impact.

Two armed men appeared in the doorway, skidding into the room. The balcony doors burst open and another man appeared with a shotgun. Reno stepped behind Skinner's chair and placed the barrel of the cocked sixgun against the colonel's temple.

'He dies first – then I kill the rest of you,' he said calmly. He shook the dazed Skinner. 'Tell 'em I can do it, Colonel.'

Skinner fumbled out a kerchief and held it to his bleeding head as he nodded jerkily. 'Clear out!' he said hoarsely. 'Out – and close the doors! Don't come unless I call you!'

The guards hesitated, but used to blind obedience left the room, closing the doors. Kincaid was slowly and painfully pulling himself on to his feet with the aid of a chair. He glared his hate at Reno, shifting his gaze to where his gun lay on the carpet.

'Grab it, Stretch,' Reno invited. 'If you want to die.'

Kincaid thought better of it, slumped forward in the chair, both hands clasped to his aching genitals. 'You're the one – gonna – die!' he gritted and Reno smiled.

'You won't do it, Stretch, and you'll need to send better men than you have done so far. Now shut up – I believe our good ol' boy is trying to say something.'

He looked at the colonel whose pale grey eyes blazed cold hate. 'You'll die, all right, Reno! But I've decided it won't be quick. I'm going to leave you be for a time. You'll never know when it's coming. You might just be starting to make something of your miserable life, feeling good about it, thinking I've let you off the hook. Then – one night, when you lest expect it–' He lifted a fat hand, index finger extended, thumb in the air, then wiggled it like a gun hammer falling. He smiled bleakly. 'Yes – I think I'll do it that way. Make you sweat a little.'

Reno shook his head, actually quite amused. 'Well, I guess that's your way, Colonel. Be a whole heap easier if you'd just accept that Elanor came with me because she saw me as a way to escape from under your thumb. I don't think she loved me or anything like that, she used me and that was OK, but–' He faltered briefly and it annoyed him that he did so. He cleared his throat. 'There was a love grew between us. I was building a home for her down near the Border, had no money and I wouldn't touch a cent of hers, so when I needed cattle, I rode down into Mexico with a few other Border ranchers to pick up some of the thousands of cattle running loose down there on one of those big Spanish ranchos. And, by the way, I'd taught her how to use a gun and she was a damn fine shot. She wasn't afraid of the loneliness – she liked it after all the years of being smothered by you.'

'But *you* got her killed no matter how you dress it up!' Skinner said viciously.

Reno nodded gently, his face changing, but he got it under control, set it in its usual hard, deadpan lines quickly. 'Yeah – we'd never had any trouble with the Comanche. It was a bunch of Reservation bucks, mad with tis-win' or some other rotgut they'd brewed and–'

'You're wrong. It was far more potent than that filthy beer they make,' cut in the colonel. 'I looked into this. It took a long time, but I found out they were drunk on rotgut likker supplied to them by a white man. And he also sold or traded them the guns they used! So while you went after the renegades and killed them all, one by one, you missed the real perpetrator!'

Reno frowned. 'I – I didn't know about him. Are you sure about this?'

Skinner smiled crookedly, triumphantly. 'See, my money you profess to despise so much does have its uses. Now get out, Reno. I'm sick of you. Just go and live with the thought that you are going to die when you least expect it – that I promise you.'

Kincaid was poised for something but there was a reluctance in his eyes that told Skinner he wasn't really ready, was still suffering from that knee between the legs...

Reno hesitated and then eased away from the colonel's chair. It was a stalemate. There was nothing he could do here. The colonel would keep his word, make his sick plans. All he could do was keep his instincts honed and his gun well-oiled and fully loaded. And live with the knowledge that the man who had really killed Elanor was still out there somewhere...

Still covering both men, he edged towards the balcony door and as he opened it and started through he paused, seeing the colonel's face suddenly light up as if with an

50

acceptable idea that had suddenly struck him.

'*Or–*' Skinner said suddenly, rising unsteadily out of his chair, his eyes glistening with an idea that had hit him with the impact of a falling tree. 'Or – I could tell you where to find the son of a bitch who sold those guns and that likker to the Comanche.' He smiled widely, cold as a bear's nose in hiberation. 'Then you could go and kill him for both of us. Maybe I'd be satisfied with that. What d'you say?'

CHAPTER 4

MISSION

Sitting at the window of the swaying car as the train rolled on through the night, Clint Reno made and lit a cigarette, staring at his dull reflection in the smoky glass.

His fair hair was tousled, longish, covering the tops of his ears. His face was long, too, narrow, like a wolf, the deep blue eyes steady and dark in their depths. His nose had been broken several times in past fights and it showed, kind of bent in the middle, hooked a little like an eagle's beak. He smiled, wide mouth thinning out some: *keep going and he would end up describing an animal, not a man,* he thought.

But above all, there was a weariness in that reflected face, a weariness that used to be combined with a resignation, a conscious decision to accept whatever life handed him and to hell with it all. But when he gazed into his own eyes again, he detected, at long last, a spark of rising interest there.

And he had the colonel to thank for that. And there was very little he had ever had to thank colonel Mason Skinner for in the years he had known the man.

But this time...

'Took me a long time to track you down, Reno,' Skinner said after Reno had come back into the big study and the colonel had ordered Kincaid out of the room, much to the sick bodyguard's chagrin. 'What were you doing down in Mexico?'

Reno knew that if the man knew he had spent almost a year south of the Border he also knew damn well what he had been doing.

After he had ridden back from the rustling raid south of the Rio and found the devastation and tragedy awaiting him at his ranch, he soon learned that other members of the wild bunch who had ridden down to steal what cattle they could had also found similar situations when they returned to their homes along the Border – but none as horrifying as his. Their families had been slaughtered but they had been shot or battered, not outraged and mutilated like Elanor, or her pet animals, cat, birds, literally torn apart. It was as if *his* ranch had been chosen for some special kind of horror...

But they had all banded together and, driven by the common rage for revenge, had set out to hunt down that bunch of renegade bucks.

The Comanche were on the run, knowing they were marked men after they had sobered up from whatever rotgut had driven them to the massacres. No one would take them in. They gathered their women and children and they ran and ran, continually hounded by the relentless white avengers. There were several clashes, the renegades scattering for safety. Most of the other whites were satisfied and returned home, saying to hell with the couple of Comanche still surviving. But Reno and one other man, Howie Rainey, who had ridden with Reno during the War, set out to make it a clean sweep.

They did, wiping out the last two Comanche bucks – and their entire families.

It was something that didn't sit easily with Reno but Rainey was unworried; he had always been the hardest man in the Ghost Troop, the biggest killer of the group that had become known as *Reno's Renegades*. Much of their reputation for utter ruthlessness had been earned because of the exploits of Howie Rainey. And one other, now dead, luckily.

They rode back to the remains of their Border spreads but Rainey was restless. He had never been married to the woman who had died in the charred ruins of his cabin, and he rode in one day and told Reno he was going down to Mexico.

'What for?' Reno felt a strong urge to get away from the place he was trying to rebuild – there were too many memories and the lonely grave on the rise above the creek haunted him because it could be seen from almost any point of the smallholding.

Rainey, a solid-built ranny with a rugged, though pleasant-enough face and large, yet delicate-looking hands, had shrugged wide shoulders. 'It was all Susannah's idea to try and settle me down. She's gone now. I liked her and I've done what I can to avenge her, but I need action, Clint. Life ain't been the same since we disbanded the *Renegades*. I've a hankerin' to get into some kinda war again and there's one down in Mexico.' He almost smiled, adding, 'There's always one down in Mexico … care to join me? You was always one for a good fight.'

It was just what Reno was looking for, although he hadn't realized it until Rainey had ridden in with his invitation. He dropped the double-bitted axe into the log he was branch-trimming and reached for his gunbelt hanging on a nearby tree.

'I'll get my gear.'

They had crossed the Rio and joined the first bunch of *revolucionarios* they met, not even asking about their 'cause' – if the Mexicans indeed had a cause, for they were all men who liked to fight for whatever reason. The rebels were mighty glad to have them join up for they were men with vast experience of battle and they trained the *revolucionarios* to a peak they could never have hoped to reach otherwise.

The leader, a self-styled General Martinez, grinned with his big teeth as victory after victory was chalked up.

''Ey, *gringos,* I think I promote you to

General but I am already General – so I make you my *Gringos Extraordinarios!* My special fighters, eh? Gold shall be yours, but if no gold, I am *en deuda,* in your debt, and I give you the whole stinking world if you ask for it, eh....?'

After several months, Reno had grown tired of the endless fighting and flight from Government soldiers who were, frankly, beginning to win more battles than they lost now. So, he quit and while Martinez didn't want him to leave, the General sighed in the end and spread his arms.

'I offer you anything and if the thing you choose is to leave, then this I grant you, with great reluctance. But we must take an oath that we will meet again one day – if we should not, then this has been a good parting, *amigo.*'

Howie Rainey had struck up a relationship with one of the Mexican women, Dolores, and elected to stay on. Reno had ridden out, drifted through northern Mexico for a spell and then returned to the United States to drift aimlessly, not knowing or caring where he went or why.

But the memory of Elanor had gone with him everywhere. The blood and powder-smoke in Mexico had failed to erase the memories – and the guilt he carried. For he knew the colonel was right – he should never have taken a woman like Elanor straight from a rich and pampered upbringing to a life on a Border hard-rock ranch…

And now the colonel had stirred some life in him, given him another chance to erase the final guilt – a man he hadn't even known still existed until last night in Skinner's study.

'The bastard's name is Peglar, Zachary Peglar,' the colonel told him, the name sounding like a bad taste in his mouth as he hunched his shoulders and leaned his elbows on his desk. 'It cost me a pretty penny to find out who had run those guns and moonshine likker to the Comanche, but Kincaid finally came up with the answer – and it took a lot more money and time to find out where the swine is right now.'

He paused, frowning now. 'What is it?'

Reno was gripping the edge of the chair, his knuckles white. His nostrils were pinched and his eyes were narrowed.

'Peglar was one of the Ghost Troop,' he said hoarsely. 'The most sadistic, loco bastard I've ever known. We had a falling-out – on one mission when we were on the run after a successful raid. The Yankees were determined to get us. We had to keep moving. We came to this farm where there was a large family, no men, only a few boys amongst the children and young women. We took most of their food and clothing and hightailed it, locking them in the house to give ourselves a little more time, but Peglar went back – and burned the house down around them.'

'Jesus! That was at Kneebone Landing, Georgia! I remember that!' The colonel stood abruptly: even at this distance from the atrocity he was unable to control his anger.

Wearily, Reno nodded. 'When we found out what Peglar had done I wanted to shoot him but we had only a few rounds between us and still a long way to go through Yankee-controlled country – so I beat him. As bad as I've ever beaten any man. He was close to death when I'd finished with him. I went a mite crazy, I guess. I knew we'd be hunted off the face of the earth now. During the fight I pushed his face into the campfire and it burned most of his hair off and mangled his left ear, ruined his eye. We left him. He eventually deserted, of course. We heard he'd been killed while riding with some of the rabble who were running wild through the South at that time. Now I know why Elanor suffered as she did. Peglar swore he'd get me, no matter how long it took … I guess this was his way.'

'Well, he's still alive, and I know where.'

'I know you're waiting for me to ask – so consider it asked,' Reno said.

Skinner snorted. 'You've lost none of your arrogance!'

Reno shook his head. 'Not arrogance, Colonel. You're just used to scaring the pants off everyone you deal with, having 'em jump through hoops because you say so. You never did faze me.'

Skinner's eyes narrowed, fat cheeks bulging up and making slits in his flesh. 'What Elanor ever saw in you I'll never know!'

'Let's not get off the subject,' Reno told him curtly. He was edgy now, shaken by the news that Peglar was still alive. He was sure he had ordered Elanor's terrible death and he knew he could not rest now until he had seen Peglar dead at his hands.

The colonel steepled his fingers, still glaring at Reno. 'All right – at this moment, Zack Peglar is at a place called Red Moon. Ever heard of it?'

'*Luna Roja* – a top-security Mexican prison, more like a fortress, southwest of Chihuahua, right over against the Sierra Madres. They call the whole area Red Moon.'

Skinner nodded slightly. 'That's the place Peglar got caught smuggling a special rifle in to someone who was going to assassinate *El Presidente,* and only because of the good relations the President's trying to build with the United States, they threw Peglar in prison for thirty years instead of putting him up against a wall and shooting him. Though there is a faction who want to do just that, in fact, I hear, including *El Presidente* himself, but he wants to do some sort of arms deal with our President so Peglar gets to live for now.' His face changed, lips curling, flesh darkening with a flood of blood through his veins and his hands clenched into fists. 'And get this – *the man lives in luxury!* He apparently has access to plenty of money and he's bought himself an apartment within Red Moon! The whole prison system's corrupt down there – it's the only way the guards, and the damn Governor himself, can make any decent money. Anyway, Peglar has a servant, I'm told, and gets his choice of women when he feels the need! The best of food prepared the way he wants it. He's safe and living high-on-the-hog and I don't intend that he should do so for much longer!'

'I think you summed it up, Colonel. The man's safe in *Luna Roja.* Out of reach.'

'That's what I thought too – no one's ever successfully busted out of Red Moon.' He leaned forward suddenly. 'And no one's ever busted *in!*'

Reno stiffened in the chair, frowning as he stared back at the hunched, intense colonel. 'What!'

Skinner eased back in his chair, his face still showing animated excitement barely contained. 'I'd thought of somehow reaching the cook who prepares Peglar's food and bribing him to poison it, but that way, he'd never know who killed him and I want him to know who and why! Now, your so-called *Renegades*. I bought a lot of information about you once I started – you and your Ghost Troop.'

'Now wait a minute!'

'Be quiet and listen! There was one mission you and your *Renegades* pulled where you broke into an exceptionally well-guarded prison and released a high-ranking Johnny-Reb officer who had important information that would have won the war for our side a lot faster if they had been able to get it out of him. Your raid was a complete success and as a result the dammed War continued for another year!'

He paused and Reno sprawled in his own chair, thrusting his long legs out in front of him now. 'Are you suggesting I gather the surviving *Reno's Renegades* and somehow break into this impregnable prison and kill Zachary Peglar?'

'Why not? You've had the experience and I know there are at least half a dozen *Renegades* still living in various parts of the country.'

'Sure, men who've put the War behind them, settled down with families. You think they're going to put their lives aside for something like this?'

'If the incentive's enough, I don't see why not.'

Reno gave him a twisted smile. 'You still think money'll buy anything, don't you?'

'Mostly it will, but in this case, because of the way the men feel about you – and Peglar – I reckon they'll agree. They practically worship you, I'm told...'

'And you think I'd trade on that?'

'I don't think you'll even have to try. I think all you'll have to do is put the deal to them and they'll agree – especially when you tell them there is the added incentive of them each earning $5,000 on the successful completion of the mission!'

'What about those who don't get out alive?'

'Then their families get the $5,000. Believe me, Reno, every one of them will agree to go with you.'

Reno's eyes were like bullets as he regarded this distasteful man. 'But *I* haven't agreed to even put the deal to them.'

Skinner showed concern, frowned deeply. 'But – you will, won't you? I know you want to see Peglar dead as much as I do now you know he's still alive. I can read you like a book, Reno – you're a born warrior. You made your try at settling down to a normal life and, God help us, it cost my daughter's life. You're drifting around now without any plan or design simply because you're restless, can't quite make up your mind to get back to where the fighting is. You might as well admit it, give into it. You know you will in the end.'

The trouble was, the colonel was right. He knew it and Clint Reno knew it – it was just a matter of coming right out and accepting the mission.

There was no choice during the War, of course, and, damn-it-to-hell, *there was no choice now!*

The colonel continued even though Reno said nothing, knowing well the man would agree eventually.

'You contact the survivors of your *Renegades,* make them the offer and sign them up. I'll pay each one a thousand dollars on acceptance, the rest after the mission's successful completion, with a guarantee their families will get the fee if they don't survive...'

He waited but Reno said nothing, just continued to look at him steadily.

'I have a ranch in southern Colorado that I can put at your disposal so that you and your men can train – I assume they'll all need to hone their various skills which must have blunted in the years since the War. Kincaid will go down ahead of time and make arrangements – you tell him what you'll need. I'll pay for all this and I want it done as quickly as possible. You'll be in charge and you can make your own arrangements about getting down to Mexico and whatever you need to do once you get there.'

'That could cost something.'

Skinner waved a hand. 'I have business interests in Mexico. I can give you letters of credit you can use to get any funds you may need. And you'll have cooperation from anyone working for me, I can guarantee that.' The colonel stood and walked to a sideboy, poured two drinks, taking one back to hand to Reno. 'I believe that should overcome all your objections.'

'Except one,' Reno said taking the drink. 'How the hell do we break into *Luna Roja?*'

'Good God, man, that's what I'm paying *you* for! I've provided all I can. You do the rest.' He clinked his glass perfunctorily against Reno's and raised it. 'Shall we drink to the success of the mission?'

Reno hesitated briefly, then raised his glass.

As he lowered his glass, the colonel said, 'Bring me Peglar's eye patch and his mangled ear as proof you've killed him.'

Reno's reflection stared back at him as the train swayed on through the night, taking him to the first of the *Renegades* – Earl Handy, his old second-in-command. Skinner had learned the man was now a freelance gambler, working any saloon circuit that would have him.

Handy had a good brain, and would be the man to figure a way to break into Red Moon or see if the mission was even feasible. He was the one man Reno felt sure would accept the deal immediately.

He was wrong.

The trouble was, when he found Earl Handy in the smoke-filled back room of a saloon in the northern New Mexico town of Wagon Mound, the man was on a winning streak and didn't want to stop or listen to any proposition for all the tea in China.

'Good to see you, Clint, but don't get between me and Lady Luck – I been chasin' her for ten years and now I finally got her cornered and I'm – gonna – be – *rich*.'

He laid out his cards, fanning them expertly on the ash-dusted, beer-stained green baize cloth of the table. 'Busted flush, gents!'

He reached through the thick smoke haze for the pile of money and then a hand came out of the fog and grabbed his wrist. Tension was a tangible thing around that table.

'Hold up, Handy! You been well-named. You're Handy, all right, handy at palmin' cards. See that Ace of spades? Well I got it's twin right here and it's been sittin' in my hand for three rounds of raisin' the pot – but one suddenly turns up to make your flush…!' The man stood, and Reno had him picked as the saloon's house man sitting in on the game. Handy might well have cheated, but Reno knew he was too smart to slip in an extra card when he didn't know where the real one was. He guessed the house man had set him up. Handy was taking too much money off the others and the saloon in general, so it was time to label him 'four-flusher' and get him thrown out on his ear – or worse.

'Earl...?' Reno said quietly. 'I'm here, pard.'

Handy didn't look at him or make any sign that he had heard. He was staring hard through the fog of smoke, and saw that the other players were ready and willing to believe the house man because they had lost a lot of money to Handy. When he spoke, he addressed the house man directly.

'You're a tinhorn liar, mister, and I'm callin' you on it!'

'Never thought you wouldn't!' crowed the house man and, partly screened by the thick layer of smoke, fired the hideaway gun he had pulled from under his flowered vest.

The bullet seared Handy's ribs and sent him staggering as the other card players dived for the floor and the house man fired again. Reno's gun came up and blasted the house man across a nearby table causing chaos and shouts as the man crashed to the floor.

But reinforcements had been waiting, confirming Reno's notion that Handy had been set up. Three men came running, guns blazing. Reno pulled Handy down to his knees but the man had his gun out now, the other hand pressed against his bleeding side. They overturned the table and a bullet chewed a splintered arc out of the edge. Then they were shooting at the running men while others were clearing out into the main part of the saloon.

Two men went down, one never to rise again, the other rolling on to his belly and shooting at Reno. He felt the wind of the slug, snapped a shot, missed, and Handy killed the man with a bullet through the head.

The remaining man had a shotgun and he brought it up confidently, but went down with his body shuddering from the hail of lead Reno and Handy pumped into him. The charge of buckshot wrecked the tinny piano in the corner, showering the cringing player with splinters and flying keys.

'Side door!' Handy gritted as more reinforcements were called for and men started towards the back room from the bar.

They scattered as the men emptied their guns at the doorway and then crashed out the side door into the night of Wagon Mound.

'Got a horse?' Reno panted, reloading on the run through an overgrown lot behind the saloon.

'No.'

'Me, neither – just came off the train. It's due to pull out again – we better make a run for it.'

'Let's go!'

Guns crashed behind them. Men were yelling. Glass shattered. Someone cursed. Someone else yelled for the pursuers to watch where the hell they were shooting.

Reno and Handy pounded their way through back alleys and heard the whistle of the train as it started to pull out of the depot. By the time they arrived, it was gathering speed, the wheels clacking over the track joints at an ever increasing rate. They were staggering, sweating, had holstered their guns now, concentrating on catching up with the train.

They burst through some brush and almost cannoned into a swaying box car. Reno leapt, snatched a handrail and scrabbled for a foothold on the narrow ledge running around the car. He held by one hand, pounded at the handle of the sliding door, freed it, kicked the edge of the door, sending it screeching back in its track.

He used the momentum of the swaying train to carry him inside. He landed, sprawling, amongst crates and sacks. Then Handy was running alongside, one hand on the edge of the juddering sliding door, reaching up with the other. Reno, gasping, sweat stinging his eyes, grabbed it and heaved, falling backwards as Earl Handy's upper body sprawled into the car. The man's legs were waving in the air and Reno crawled forward, bunched up the back of the man's coat and dragged him all the way in.

They fell in a tangled heap and lay there for several minutes, getting their breath as the train's speed increased and the whistle screamed one final time as they cleared the outskirts of Wagon Mound.

In the dimness of the car, as the sliding door banged back and forth in the track, Reno saw the flash of Handy's teeth in the well-known reckless smile.

'Now, about this deal...' the gambler gasped, holding a crumpled kerchief over his bleeding side.

CHAPTER 5

A GATHERING OF WOLVES

Reno had never met Craig Enderby's wife before but he knew right off they weren't going to get along.

At Craig's small spread, she looked up from raking hay in the back of the rickety barn, pushed some strands of wheat-coloured hair off her face and stared at Reno with no welcome at all in her beautiful lavender eyes.

'So you're the famous Lieutenant Reno,' she said flatly when Craig made the introductions. 'I've been dreading your arrival.'

That caught Reno off-guard. He hadn't announced his coming; he had just turned up when Earl Handy told him where Enderby's spread was. 'Don't quite understand, Loretta.'

She drove the hayfork into a pile and dusted off her hands before placing them on her nicely-curved hips. 'I know your type, Lieutenant–'

'Just mister, ma'am.'

'Oh, but you still think of yourself as the rakehell lieutenant, don't you...?'

'Hey, Loretta, what's the matter with you? Clint's an old friend. He saved my life more than once,' Craig Enderby said, looking and sounding a little worried at the woman's attitude.

'Of course he did! And you feel beholden to him. The "old friend from the army days", stirring up the old memories and now come to disrupt our lives!'

Reno was mighty uncomfortable. So far, everything the damn woman had said was close to the truth if not right on.

'Clint just happened to be in the general area and he's been speakin' with another old army friend, Earl Handy, who told him where our place is... For God's sake, Loretta!'

Her cool gaze bored into Reno's rugged face. 'Is that right, Lieutenant? You just – happened by?'

'Not exactly,' Reno admitted slowly and she smiled.

'I thought not. Well, you have your talk with Craig in privacy. There'll be coffee up at the house if you'd care for some before you go.'

'Loretta!'

72

She smiled again, meaninglessly, and went out of the barn. Craig started after her but Reno took his arm and shook his head slowly.

'She's right, Craig. I didn't just happen by.' Enderby frowned and Reno added, 'I'm getting the old *Renegades* together. There's a job for us down in Mexico that pays $5,000.'

Craig Enderby blinked. It made him look even younger and he already had boyish features to start with.

'Lordy, lordy. I could sure use some of that money!' He gestured around him but Reno had already noted the rundown state of the spread, the few very ordinary cattle, the small and inadequate creek.

'A thousand down when you sign on, the rest after the job's done successfully.'

'And what if it ain't done successfully?'

Reno hesitated. 'I'm not sure. You'd get to keep the thousand anyway, I think. But if the worst should happen–'

'You mean if I got killed.'

'Yeah – well, your wife would get the balance of the money.'

'Guaranteed?'

Again, just a slight hesitation before answering.

'Guaranteed. It's Colonel Skinner, my father-in-law, who's backing the deal.' Reno went on to tell what had happened with Elanor and it shook Craig considerably.

'So that sunuver Peglar is still alive!' Craig said. 'Well, I'd come if for no other reason than to see that scum dead, but like I say, I could sure use money. I – I ain't provided too well for Loretta. It gets her down at times.'

'That's OK. I savvy that.'

'Well, count me in, Clint.' They shook hands. 'Er – you want to come up to the house for that cup of java?'

Reno smiled ruefully. 'Wouldn't be game not to, Craig.'

They laughed and walked up to the small house with the missing shingles, the broken drainpipe and the water pump that lay in several pieces on a square of burlap where Craig had been working on it.

Loretta Enderby poured the coffee and slid a cup across the kitchen table where Reno sat. Craig was talking fast and enthusiastically about the deal Reno had offered and the woman kept moving about the kitchen, took some freshly baked biscuits and placed them on a plate on the table.

'Well, the money would be welcome, but I don't want you to go, Craig.'

'Look, my darlin', we badly need the dough and this is only for a few weeks, couple of months at most. We could never hope to get $5,000 out of this place in ten years!'

She held up her hand. 'Oh, I know you'll go anyway. It makes sense in a way – but I still don't want you to go.' She glared now at Reno. 'Damn you, Lieutenant Reno! I wish you'd finish your coffee and go! You're not welcome here!'

She stormed out of the kitchen into another part of the house and Reno heard a door slam dully somewhere.

'Listen, Craig, I don't want to break up your marriage. Maybe it'll be best if...'

'If I take the job, that's what'll be best, Clint – anyway, we shook hands on it, didn't we? She's right, you know. The pull of the old days is pretty strong.'

Reno nodded slowly. 'I know. If you'll ride into town with me to your bank, I'll have that thousand dollars paid into your account.'

Craig chuckled. 'What account? That's how bad we need the dough, Clint. What money we have is in a coffee can on that there shelf and it don't even cover the bottom!'

Jimmy Udo wouldn't be joining the old *Renegades.* Reno knew this as soon as he saw the man sitting in a rocker on the porch of his parents' ranch house in Lando, Georgia.

The man had lost both legs in a wagon overturn several years ago. He was bitter and a drunk, and his red-eyed father and work-worn sister who cared for him hit Reno for some money anyway.

He gave them a hundred dollars of his own and just as he was leaving, Jimmy singing old Army songs with a raucous bitterness, the man threw up all down his front and his sister raged at him like a harridan. It shook Reno – all that filthy invective coming out of that small, worn-out woman.

He rode out hastily with Jimmy Udo's drunken laughter ringing in his ears.

And he thought he had problems...

He found Cole Gannon in a travelling medicine show, taking on all comers in the boxing tent, using lead weights inside his gloves or spilling Lysol over them and half blinding his opponents, or sometimes slip-ping chicken wire under the padding so it protruded through the leather covering and opened up bad cuts on the challenger's face. The referee would step in quickly to stop the fight and declare Gannon the winner on a technical knock-out.

'Gotta do it, Clint,' Gannon told Reno in the back of the sweat-and-liniment-smelling tent. 'The boss don't aim to pay out no twenty-five bucks to some hayseed who thinks because he can knock his wife across the room he can beat the tar out of his champion–' He turned a crooked thumb towards his chest, grinning and showing the broken, gapped teeth. 'Yours truly.'

'Well, you always did throw a mean punch, Cole – without the gloves and whatever else you stick inside 'em.'

Gannon squinted. His face was battered, his nose hammered over to one side, the flesh around his lips and eyes scarred. He'd once been quite good looking and something of a ladies' man.

'I hear a sneakin' disapproval there, Loot?'

Reno smiled, shrugging. 'Just took me by surprise. Thought you were going back to the shooting circuit after the War, gonna take all the prize money around.'

Gannon's face straightened. He spat suddenly, making Reno step back quickly. 'Yankees killed that idea. No Reb was allowed a firearm, under Reconstruction, you recall. I got caught at one turkey-shoot and they threw me on a chain gang for two years, beat the stuffin' outta me. Guns were easier to come by when I got out but I never did no good at the target shoots – seem to've lost it. Along with some of my teeth and about forty-five pounds while on the chain gang. Then I got into a street brawl one day and the boss' – he gestured vaguely towards the front of the big fighting tent where a man's hoarse voice was urging the local lads to challenge The Great Gannon and win twenty-five crisp new dollar notes – 'the boss seen me, paid my fine and told me he'd put me to work in his fightin' troupe. Of course, the fine came outta my first wages but he ain't so bad. Tight with a dollar but won't let a man starve and takes care to see I don't get too badly hurt with some of these high steppin' pugs. Now and again he rigs the bets, of course.'

'You can do better than this, Cole.'

Gannon shrugged. 'Kind of gotten into the habit now. We get around, see a lot of country. I always was restless you might recall.'

'Restless and one of the best rifle shots I've ever seen. In fact, best shot with anything – rifle, sixgun, shotgun, catapult, even an Indian bow.'

'Aw, that was a long time ago, Clint.' Gannon wouldn't meet his gaze. He seemed ashamed.

'Booze a problem?' Reno asked straight out and Gannon's right fist came up cocked, ready to beat his head in. But Reno didn't flinch, looked steadily into the murky eyes. 'I can smell it on your breath, Cole. And I saw those empties under your bed.'

Gannon shrugged, slowly lowering the fist. 'Like I said, I've gotten used to a lot of things.'

'Man like you is born with the kind of talent you had, Cole. It's still there. Needs drawing out again, is all...'

'Leave it go, Clint! Told you – I'm happy enough here.'

'How much happier would $5,000 make you? And a chance to go on another mission with the *Renegades?*'

Gannon stiffened. His broken face started to sag but he swallowed, got control quickly enough, ran a tongue over battered, swollen lips. 'This gospel, Clint?' Reno merely continued to look at him and Gannon nodded. 'Yeah – 'course it is. Just a minute.'

He pushed past Reno and went through to the front of the tent where the boss of the boxing troupe was encouraging a large local lad who was also being urged on by his friends to accept the challenge.

'Man, I ought to turn you down,' the boss was saying. He was a hard-faced, gimlet-eyed shyster with no neck, only thick shoulders busting the seams of his dirty shirt. 'I let you fight my man and I'm gonna lose twenty-five bucks, I can tell.'

'He could be right, friend,' Gannon said suddenly, stepping out on to the raised platform, his presence bringing the boss's head snapping around.

The promoter rounded quickly on Gannon.

'The hell're you doin' out here! Git back inside till I call you…'

'Just wanted the laddie to see what he'll be up against, boss,' Gannon said brightly and the tone of the man's voice as much as his words brought a puzzled frown to the boss's face. Gannon turned to the big local man who reeked of beer. 'Feller, you could walk into a straight right – like this!' And his fist smashed into the middle of the startled promoter's face, knocking him halfway across the platform. Gannon danced after him, fists raised. 'Or a left hook like this. Aw, geez, boss, lemme help you up off your knees. There, hold steady now while I demonstrate my uppercut.'

They heard the boss's teeth crash together even at the back of the cheering crowd. The promoter's head snapped back and his feet all but lifted off the platform and then he crumpled to his knees, falling against Gannon's thick legs. The fighter knocked the man's derby hat off, twisted his fingers in the lank hair and pulled so the man's bleeding, slack face was raised.

''Course, the boss don't allow me to hit a man when he's down – I mean, none of this slammin' a hammerblow into his face. Or flingin' him face down on the floor, like this! But you get the right idea. Anyway, friend, I don't guess we'll ever find out if you could beat me or not, because I just quit.'

He stepped over the prone and bloody promoter and went back into the tent, followed by the crowd's cheers. Reno looked at him quizzically as Gannon sucked a throbbing knuckle. 'Take me two minutes to get my things together.'

'Cole – leave the booze. You're on the wagon from here on in.'

That stopped Gannon in his tracks for a moment and he looked longingly at the part-empty whiskey bottle protruding from under his pillow. Then he straightened, lifting a slim warbag and nodded, sniffing loudly.

'Let's go, Clint. I'm ready to start livin' again.'

Reno wanted a man named Red Rogan

back on the team but when he reached the town where the man was supposed to be and enquired, the sheriff offered to take him to Rogan.

He was in an unmarked grave in a back corner of the town's Boot Hill.

'Never knew who he was,' the sheriff said, pointing to the blank pine headboard. 'I'll have his name painted on. He was hell-fast with a sixgun but a feller rode in was just that little bit faster. Day before yesterday.'

'There's always someone that little bit faster,' mused Reno and handed the sheriff some money. 'Get a headstone put on the grave. I'll give you Red's details.'

'Sure he's worth it? I mean, he was just a drifter on the prod...'

'I'll ride back through this town one of these days. That headstone better be in place with what I tell you carved on it.'

The lawman's eyes narrowed and then he pocketed the money, and nodded. 'You'll get what you want, mister – I'll be lookin' for you.'

'You'll see me – sometime.'

The sheriff smiled crookedly. 'I just bet I will – might even let you buy me a drink.'

'Might even do that.'

Reno rode out soon after. He had one

more call to make to complete the team.

He wasn't surprised to find Hondo King in jail.

The man was almost ten years older than any of the other *Renegades* but he was a hell-raiser and more trouble than the young bucks had been when they tied a can to the tail of the curly wolf after a mission.

He wasn't a large man, but he was a fine gunsmith when he wasn't getting into trouble over women, and he could fight like a thrashing machine in a field of wind-blown wheat when he started. And he would start at the drop of a hat – or a word that didn't sit right with him.

Didn't matter who said the word; size, age, even gender at times, didn't count. If Hondo took offence someone was going to lose some teeth. Sometimes it was Hondo, but he always seemed to come back for more and was a hard man to keep down.

'How you been keepin', Clint?' Hondo greeted Reno through the bars of the cell, just as if he had seen the man only a day or two earlier instead of almost ten years ago.

'Tolerable, Hond. What'd you do this time?'

'Aw, her husband come back unexpected and somehow or other he fell or was kinda pushed through the front window of his store. He'll live but he's gonna have a lot of fancy hemstitchin' accordin' to the sawbones.'

'Sheriff tells me you've got to pay the man's medical bills and repairs to his store – and his wife's clothes. She claims you tried to rape her...'

Hondo pulled at the lobe of one ear. 'Yeah, well, that's OK – I don't want to get her into more trouble. I don't have but a few bucks so I guess it's time on the chain gang for me.'

'Not necessarily – that's if you'd like to hitch up with the *Renegades* again and do a little job south of the Border.'

Hondo showed real interest now. 'Oh, man! I could sure do with a taste of that Mexican chili! I ain't had any gen-u-ine stuff for years!'

Reno knew the *chili* Hondo referred to was not the bowl of throat-searing soup they served in *cantinas*. It was more *who* served it that interested Hondo King.

'You'll have to go to Colorado and get into training with the boys – there'll be guns for you to work on.'

'What's the pay?'

Reno smiled – Hondo was in.

The nearest town to the colonel's ranch in the far south-west of Colorado was Cortez. It was not far from that corner in the Ute Mountains that was the only point in the US common to four States – Colorado, New Mexico, Arizona and Utah. There was a Southern Ute Reservation on the Colorado-New Mexico Line and a Navajo Reserve across the western line in Utah. It was almost in the shadow of the Mesa Verde and Reno suspected that the colonel had some private reason for keeping the ranch going, other than raising cattle, which were only of average quality.

Whatever it was, he knew he would never find out and in truth, wasn't much interested. He knew the colonel's wealth hadn't all come from legitimate dealings.

He stopped in Cortez on the way out to the ranch, known as Cross S – a brand that consisted of a large 'X' with an 'S' entwining the arms. In the Four Corners' area it was simply called 'The Colonel's Place'.

By now the rest of the team ought to have arrived. He had given each member rail fare as far as Dunango and then it was up to them how they made their way out to the Cross S.

He aimed to stay overnight in town,

having hired a buckboard to take his supplies with him – these consisted of cases of weapons sent down by Skinner as well as food and harness and tools.

He made arrangements with the freighter to store the loaded buckboard in his warehouse overnight. He would bring a hire team from the livery to hitch up the next morning.

It was while he was hitching up the team that a girl's voice called to him by name.

'Mr Clint Reno?'

He turned and stared at the young woman standing a few feet away in the dusty warehouse shed, the sun at her back, outlining her long-legged slim figure in Levis with buckskin halfboots. She wore a checkered shirt, a hat with a rawhide chinstrap – and a Colt in .36 calibre holstered high on her left side for a cross draw.

That intrigued Reno and he stared at it for a long minute before looking at the rest of her. Nice shape, he allowed, curved and softly so at that. Hair ablaze with the sun behind it, a rich, deep red, face oval, tanned, with a small nose and mouth. He knew the eyes had to be green with hair like that but he couldn't see them clearly to be sure.

'I'm Reno.'

She stepped forward, holding out a gloved

hand. 'My name's Lucky Cornell – I'm Red Rogan's twin sister and I'm here to take his place in whatever mission you and your *Renegades* are going on. Would you like a hand to harness the team...?'

CHAPTER 6

READY!

As the woman made to lift the traces he stepped between her and the buckboard.

'Hold up! Who'd you say you were? Lucy...?'

'*Lucky* – well, Lucinda, actually, which gradually went through "Lucy" and ended up as "Lucky". I have been pretty lucky in my life, too.'

'And what gives you a different name to Red Rogan? Cornell, isn't it?'

'That's the family name. Red took the "Rogan" when he joined the army. He lied about his age, of course.'

Reno remembered Red had been mighty young when he had first appeared in his troop. 'You know he's dead?' he asked gently.

She nodded, sober now. 'So I learnt when I went to meet him in Emerson Creek... I'm afraid he had a hair trigger temper to go with his red hair. And he'd always been the fastest with his gun – until a week or so ago.'

He studied her now and saw a definite resemblance to how he remembered Red. 'Twins, eh?'

'Not identical, but like all twins we were close. Red got your wire to say you'd meet him in Highset, but he was going to meet me first in Emerson Creek and we planned to ride to Highset together.'

'Well, when he didn't turn up I went to Emerson Creek, it being the closest town, thinking he might've been held up.'

She nodded and said very quietly, 'Yes.' He heard the catch in her voice, saw the glimmer of filling tears in her eyes but she looked away, draped the traces over the edge of the buckboard.

'After I learnt what had happened to him, I knew you'd be a man short – so here I am to take Red's place.'

'Uh-uh.' He shook his head to emphasize the refusal.

'Why? You think because I'm a woman that I can't ride and shoot–' She stepped back and he threw himself aside as her gloved hand streaked across her body and then the .36 calibre Navy Colt was blasting in two shots very close together. He heard a *thunk!* from a plank across the other side of the livery and saw a fresh hole there, a narrow light shaft angling down through the dust motes floating in the air.

Annoyed that he had reacted like a frightened fool, Reno stood, brushing down his trousers as the hostler poked his head around a corner. Reno waved down the aisle to him. 'It's OK.' He turned to the girl. 'Two shots, but I only see one hole.' *Damned* if he was going to act impressed.

Then she said casually, 'I put the two bullets through the same knothole.'

He allowed his scepticism to show on his face. She leaned down to the top of her right boot and straightened. Something flashed in her hand and a slim blade with a flat handle wound with a strip of rawhide quivered in the plank next to the bullet hole. 'Right about there you'll see where it went through just a little off-centre.'

Frowning, Reno walked across slowly, watching her. By God, she was right! The right hand edge of the knothole, closest to where the knife still quivered a little in the wood, showed a gouge where the second bullet had gone through – slightly off-centre as she claimed.

He walked back to her looking thoughtful. 'Why would you want to join the *Renegades?*'

'Why wouldn't I? I've been hearing about them ever since the end of the War. Red was always singing the praises of Lieutenant Clint Reno and he mentioned others, too, who had impressed him – Howie Rainey, I believe, an older man named Hondo. I've heard all about your exploits behind enemy lines, Reno, I wanted to meet you. That's why I was going to come see you with Red.'

He didn't know what to say, and finally shrugged. 'Well, you've met me.'

'And I want to meet the rest of the team.'

'This isn't a reunion of old soldiers, you know.'

'Red suspected as much. He was quite excited, looking forward to – re-grouping, I believe he called it?'

Reno pursed his lips. Deciding, he said quietly, 'We're going down to Mexico. There'll be fighting.'

'I hope so.'

'Look, what in the hell is this? I can't take you and you know it. I'm glad to have met you and I'm sorry Red was killed in that shoot-out, but this is one time you're *un*lucky – or maybe *lucky,* depending on how you look at it.'

'I look at it as standing in on my brother's behalf – it's what he would want me to do. We've always fought each other's battles, right through school and into adulthood. I need to do this, Reno. I loved Red and now he's gone and this is something I can do in his name and you can't damn well stop me!'

'Well, I dunno know about that.' But Reno knew he was only stalling. She could shoot and she could handle a knife and he had no doubt that she could ride and rope well, but there was still the fact that she was a *woman.* She might feel she owed Red something, but, damnit, *he* owed Red something too: he had to look out for Red's sister now and taking her down to Mexico with the rest of the *Renegades* – well, hell, he just couldn't do it, could he...?

'I'll follow you even if you don't let me join you,' she said and he exploded.

'Goddammit-to-hell, woman! What the blazes d'you think you're playing at? This isn't a game! We're going to be dodging bullets, living with Mexican rebels who are little better than cut-throat *bandidos.* We're going to have to ride through a hundred miles of some of the roughest country on the continent and at the end we're going to have the toughest job we've ever been asked to do waiting for us.'

'I can speak fluent Spanish, did I mention that?'

He glared. 'No! You didn't mention that – and likely there're lots of other things you didn't mention, but *it doesn't damn well matter!* Because you're not coming!'

Suddenly her green eyes were like the ice rimming a high-mountain stream on a winter's morn. 'You can't stop me riding down to Mexico if I want to – and I'll shoot anyone who tries. Maybe not fatally but certainly it will hurt a lot. I'm good at placing bullets exactly where I want them to go.' She smiled dazzlingly, startling him. 'Our father was a good teacher – Red must have told you where he learned to shoot so well...?'

Reno continued to hold her gaze and then nodded gently. 'Yeah, he did – mentioned you, come to think of it now. Look, I can see you're dead-set to do this. You'll be a lot safer riding with the rest of us but I still can't let you join in the fighting.'

The smile stayed as she said maddeningly, 'You just try and stop me. By the way, did I tell you I'm an excellent cook...?'

He threw up his hands. 'You must have

strong arms.'

She frowned, puzzled.

'I mean, it's a wonder you don't break 'em – patting yourself on the back the way you do.'

She merely blew him a kiss and laughed softly. 'Let's get the wagon ready for the trail, shall we? Oh, I'm good at first aid, too. Now that might come in handy, wouldn't you say...? And horses seem to like me and–'

'Enough! You can come! Jesus! *You – can – come!*'

She smiled again. 'I never doubted it for a second.'

She was an asset. She could do everything she claimed and was a bright friendly person into the bargain. Only Hondo mistook her friendliness for something he might exploit, but he found out that Lucky Cornell was more than a handful.

He made his pass at her when she was dishwashing in the lean-to behind the big dog-run where the meals were served on the ranch, slipping up behind her, placing his hands on her hips and pulling her back against him.

Moments later he was spluttering and cursing, clawing soapy water out of his eyes, drenched with the hot washing-up water.

And then it seemed as if a bunch of wildcats had jumped him as he was kicked and punched and his hair was pulled and he was flung head-first against the log wall before sinking sickly to his knees. The racket had brought the others from the supper table and they were just in time to see Lucky place a boot against the hunched-over Hondo's shoulder and thrust him roughly to the ground. She placed her boot on his chest, leaned down, and the whisper of cold steel sliding out of the boot sheath froze Hondo – and the onlookers – as she placed the blade beside his eye.

'I can blind you or cut off a finger or two or even cut your throat – or worse. But I don't think I need to. You won't paw me again, will you?'

'Not me!' Hondo gasped. 'I wasn't gonna–'

He stopped as the blade pressed into his flesh, pricking it so a bead of blood appeared on his throat.

'Don't bother, Hondo. We both know what you were about. Just let it end here while you'll still got your manhood intact.'

He waved his hands quickly. 'Whatever you say lady!'

She sheathed the blade and smiled as she

offered her small hand and helped him to his feet. She looked around at the others. 'He must be getting old – slipped on the wet floorboards. He's all right now, aren't you, Hondo?'

'I'm – fine,' he murmured and walked away, boots squelching with the soapy water that had run down inside them.

Lucky Cornell never had any trouble with any of the men after that. Not that she couldn't have handled it if she did...

Not all of the re-activated *Renegades* had lost their skills in the ten years since the end of the War.

Hondo King was still as skilful as ever with his gunsmithing and recommended that Reno change the brand new Winchester '73 rifles for carbines. The shorter barrels would be better for the type of raid they were planning. He also undertook to reshape the firing pins which he considered to be too rounded on the striker end, a meticulous, time-consuming job, but Kincaid had managed to obtain all the tools and equipment he needed.

Hondo also recommended that they load some ammunition for themselves instead of using the factory bullets which were always somewhat old before they hit the stores of the Western frontier.

'Increase the powder by seven grains,' he said to Earl Handy whose job it was to reload the brass cartridge cases. 'The case will stand it easily and the brass'll expand quicker, seal better in the breech, and send the bullet on a flatter trajectory. A little faster, too, but the speed's not so important as accuracy.'

Handy himself was still as adept as ever with his guns and Reno put him in charge of the target shooting as well as the reloading.

'You won't believe who's the best shot,' he said to Reno one evening after a day on the shooting range, built by the Cross S ranch hands under Kincaid's supervision, way back in a draw north of the ranch house. 'That damn gal! Never seen such an eye. Don't waste any time, neither. Lifts that Winchester, sights and *bam!* There goes the bull, over and over. Never seen anyone like it – except maybe for Gannon, but he uses a telescopic sight and that rolling-breach Remington single-shot. You'd expect tack-drivin' accuracy from such an outfit, but the gal does it with a factory weapon!'

'Looks like it was lucky we hired – Lucky,' Reno said with a crooked smile.

Craig Enderby always seemed worried and Reno surmised, correctly that he was worrying about Loretta at home. But he was a good physical fitness instructor and wore out most of the group on long runs, sometimes with burlap sacks full of rocks strapped to their backs, up into the hills behind the big ranch. He took them for dangerous night rides, climbing in the rugged hills, had them sliding down ropes on vertical cliff faces, climbing the same ropes on the same cliffs, almost wrenching their arms out of the sockets if you could believe the bitching of the men.

Reno suspected he was getting himself in shape, both mentally and physically, and this was why he drove the others, including Reno, so hard.

Reno himself took them out into the wilderness of the hills and taught them survival skills: most remembered instinctively but he wanted them properly honed. There was every chance that even if they pulled off the raid on *Luna Roja* successfully that they would have to scatter and make their own ways back to the Rio. And there was a lot of wild, danger-ridden country between Red Moon and the Border.

What the cowboys who worked the place thought of it all was anybody's guess, but Kincaid had warned them to keep their mouths shut about the goings-on at Cross S.

'You do what you're told and the colonel will see you right. He mentioned a bonus after it's all over and you know he can be generous when he wants to be.'

And a goddamn piker when he doesn't, Reno thought but kept it to himself.

He and Kincaid seemed to mutually avoid each other. It wasn't that either was afraid, just that there was a job to be done in as fast a time as possible and they knew if they clashed there would be a fight that might end in real bloodshed, and that wouldn't suit anybody – least of all the colonel.

So they got by with a kind of armed truce between them and the days edged on into weeks, and by the end of a month, the *Renegades* reckoned they were about as good as they were going to get.

'We'll give it one more week,' Reno told them to a chorus of groans. 'We need more night work. From what Kincaid tells me, it's open plain right up to Red Moon so looks to me like we'll be doing some night riding. We've got to get down there and make contact with Martinez and Howie Rainey and the *revolucionarios* yet. So, next time I hear you say "ready", I want you to mean it.'

Ten days later Reno was satisfied with their

fitness and reaction times and one morning he announced at breakfast that they would be leaving for Mexico at sundown.

'Might as well get used to night riding. We'll swim the Rio, dodge the offical crossing points – so, let's go!'

There were mules to be loaded – there were spare weapons and a couple of cases of dynamite to be taken south with them. Mules would be far better in the country they had to travel than a buckboard, although it would be easier to carry their load in the latter.

But Reno didn't want to go to the *revolucionarios* empty-handed. After all, he was going to need their backing if they were to have any chance at all of pulling off this deal.

Kincaid handed Reno the maps and a rough plan of the prison itself. His face was hard. 'You better pull this off.'

'You gonna lose sleep over it if I don't?'

Kincaid grinned tightly. 'Hell, no. If you make a mess of it I know you'll be dead, and I'll dance on your grave – if I can find it after Governor Vega finishes with you. He'll likely scatter your bits and pieces all over the countryside!'

'*Gracias,* Kincaid. That's just the kind of farewell I need.'

'*Por nada,* you son of a bitch!'

CHAPTER 7

REBEL ROUSER

Two days earlier, they had made a successful night crossing of the border into Mexico and Reno led them deep into the hills of the Continental Divide, keeping to the wild trails. They skirted the small towns of Nogales and Ascension, crossed the Casa Grande between Janos and Fernandez Leal, rode the ragged brushlands and re-crossed the Casa Grande south of Dublan and cut across the Santa Maria at Galeana.

Here Reno left them camped in a hidden canyon while he rode up into the rugged hills of the Sierra de las Tunas. This was where General Martinez and his band had holed up previously. Their main camp had been there, although they had others scattered right across Mexico's largest State of Chihuahua. The *revolucionarios* all across Mexico were on the run now, fugitives, hunted down by Government troops, the rebel leaders either gone to ground or fled the country to the *Estados Unidos* or south to the mid-Americas.

Fact was, he didn't even know if Martinez and his men were still fighting their war or had turned into nothing more than *bandidos,* harassing Government wagons, trains and small troops of soldiers, even travellers who might have a poke of gold or a few spare pesos hidden in their clothing.

It had happened to a lot of other rebels who could no longer fight the overwhelming strength of *El Presidente*'s forces.

All Reno had to go on was that Howie Rainey hadn't returned to the US, and he knew the man would have if he had grown tired of Dolores or had become bored with a lack of fighting. So he called up landmarks from his memory of his time down here, and a couple of days after leaving the *Renegades* in the hidden canyon was challenged by a stubbled, ragged peon standing on a high rock above the trail. *Makes a damn fine target, the loco fool,* Reno thought, as he hauled rein and lifted an arm to indicate he came in peace.

'It is Reno, *amigo.* General Martinez's *xtraordinario gringo* the compadre of Señor Rainey.'

Silence and then, *'Eh! Reno amigo!* Here is

Miguel Boca. We once share the same serape in the snows of the Madres – you remember?'

'I remember, Miguel – I had flea bites for two weeks afterwards!'

The guard's laugh echoed amongst the rocks. '*Sí* me, too – and in the most inconvenient places, eh? Ride *amigo*. It will be agreeable to shake your hand once more.'

After they met and shook hands and exchanged a few more reminiscences, Reno asked, 'The general, and Señor Rainey – they are still here?'

'Oh, *sí, sí* – but is boring times, *amigo,* believe me. There are too many Government troops and too many *revolucionarios* kiss the scarred wall in *Luna Roja.*'

Reno tensed. 'The general has men imprisoned in Red Moon?'

'Too many of our *amigos,* Reno. We are but a small force now. Sometimes numbering twenty, sometimes less, depending on the devil's whim. *Aiy, yi,* that Governor Bega of the Red Moon, he scourge our country, capture many men, kill many others and their families, anyone who helped the rebels. There is a handful of pesos for any man who turns us in and there are many empty bellies in Chihuahua, Reno. So...' He shrugged.

Reno nodded. So Vega, the State Governor and also in charge of the prison, was terrorizing the country, capturing the rebels where he could, imprisoning them for torture before putting them against the scarred wall for execution.

'Take me to the general, Miguel. I think I have some news that will please him.'

'That will be *muy bueno, amigo! Muy bueno!* I get my horse and soon you will see your friend Rainey again. Dolores is with child and I think Rainey will leave us soon.'

Reno smiled: sounded like Howie Rainey hadn't changed a hell of a lot.

It was a big welcome as Reno had anticipated and the general wouldn't even listen as to why he was here. He was simply happy to see him, and they brought in a big red deer shot by Miguel Boca in the hills and soon the festivities were under way.

'Didn't expect to see you down this way again, Clint,' Howie Rainey said, passing around a bottle of the tequila Reno had brought with the supplies.

Rainey had lost some weight, was leaned way down, looked gaunt and not so boisterous as in the past. Maybe it was the daunting prospects of imminent fatherhood.

'Tell you later when we can get the general

in a listening mood. But for now, start thinking about the Red Moon prison.'

'Oh-oh,' Rainey said and there was a sudden gleam in his eye. 'Do I smell action?'

'Five thousand bucks' worth for you and the general – the others will average a couple of hundred pesos.'

Rainey whistled softly. 'Small fortune to these fellers. Five grand makes it sound like a tough deal.'

'Likely it will be. I need to send someone for the old *Renegades* team. I left them in Minero Canyon.'

'I'll send Ramon – he's a fast rider.'

The others arrived by nightfall, in time to join in the wild skirt-swinging, toe-tapping dancing and the singing of bawdy Spanish songs and the general air of fiesta. There was much laughter, plenty to eat and drink – and a lot of sore heads come morning.

Reno found the general snoring in his bed-roll with the slim arms of a buxom *señorita* flung across his barrel chest. He opened one red eye and curled up one corner of his mouth – it might have been the beginnings of a smile.

'When you're ready, General,' Reno told Martinez. 'We've some business to discuss.'

Martinez groaned and waved a hand.

'Later, *amigo.*'

'Sorry, General. This has to be done and I need your help.'

'Ah – then that is different. One hour – just give me one hour and we will put away our smiles and hangovers and talk business…'

He slapped the girl on her naked buttocks, pulled the cover over them again and waved Reno away.

Reno shook his head slowly as he walked off and saw Lucky Cornell sitting on a log, smoking a cigarillo. He sat beside her and made a cigarette.

'You seemed to enjoy yourself last night. Saw you handle a few wandering hands pretty good.'

'I was always a tomboy – Pa used to say we might have been twin brothers instead of brother and sister. Reno, these people seem so poor and yet they throw a great welcome party. And just look at the fancy rags they get around in.'

He smiled, pointing to the mouth of a small cave up the slope from the main camp. 'Look in there and you'll find chests of clothes they've taken from travellers, looted somewhere.' As he fired up a match and dipped the end of his cigarette into it he added, 'The general saw you dancing last night. He mentioned he thought you should have a man of your own.'

She did not smile. 'I choose my own men in my own good time, Reno. You might remember that – and pass it along to the general. And anyone else who might wish to poke their nose into my business.'

She gave him the steady eye and he flicked an eyebrow and nodded slowly. 'I reckon you can look after yourself, Lucky.'

'You believe that.'

She tossed the half-smoked cigarillo into the coals of the fire, picked up a piece of cooked but cold venison and began to chew as she moved away. Reno watched her go. *One tough lady – and he wouldn't want to tangle with her.*

The general liked the idea of making a move against *Luna Roja.*

'Ai-yiii-yiii! The Red Moon will set soon, eh, *gringo mio,* eh? That Vega, he round up many of my friends and throw them in his stinking jail and he pull their fingernails and burn their *cojónes* and put out their eyes and then he shoot them. It is said he has vowed to paint the scarred wall with the blood of *revolucionarios* by the time winter comes.' He spat. 'I like to get my hands on this Governor Vega, but he lives behind the walls of his fortress with his *rubia,* the golden-haired mistress called Madonna. He surrounds himself with plenty of guards. He is like – king, emperor. He is in charge of the Red Moon Region and is law only to himself. He say do somet'ing, and it is done or someone's throat is–' He made a cutting gesture from ear to ear with one dark finger. 'Ah, *sí,* you tell us how and we take this *Luna Roja* and I have the pleasure of dealing with this Vega, eh?'

Reno's face straightened. 'I was hoping you might have some notion of how to get in there, General.'

The general looked disappointed as he shook his head. 'Ah, *hijo de la puta!*' he cursed slapping a hand against his forehead. 'I think and think for long time. Rainey, my other *gringo extraordinario,* he think too. We never find way.'

'I rode down to take a look at that *Luna Roja,* Clint,' Rainey spoke up. 'We've lost a lot of men to Vega, like the general said. He roped in a lot of rebels and is still slaughtering them when the whim takes him.'

'What's the place like?' Reno asked a mite impatiently.

'Like a damn fortress. Built close to a sheer cliff at the rear, has big pits dug all round and only one way to get in across a bridge at the front. You ain't gonna believe this but it's a drawbridge, like in some of them old English castles.'

'You're kidding.'

'Sorry, Clint, but that's how it is. The bridge is down most of the day, hauled up at night, but there's only treeless plains on the approaches. They say it was originally built by Maximilian for some sort of summer retreat – it's quite a bit cooler in the foothills of the Madres where it's located. But when he came to an end, so did Red Moon and *El Presidente* turned it into an impregnable prison.'

'There must be some way in.'

'Likely there is, for maybe one or two men. But what the hell good could they do?'

'Lower the drawbridge for others waiting outside, maybe,' suggested Reno.

'Where they gonna wait?' Rainey answered impatiently. 'Just got through tellin' you there's no cover on that approach…'

'Then they have to wait in the open but look harmless and innocent.'

They all swung their gazes towards Lucky Cornell as she spoke up.

'Well, it's obvious, isn't it? If there's nowhere to hide you just have to ride right on up and hammer on the front door.'

Someone snorted. 'Typical woman. Duck

all the problems, just says "go ahead and do it" and never mind the details.' It was Hondo King but Lucky didn't even look at him. She was watching the general, Rainey and Reno.

'Well, the idea sounds OK,' allowed Reno. 'Doing it's another thing, though, Lucky.'

'I know it won't be easy – and like Hondo says, there are many details, but if there's no other way, sometimes the direct approach is all that's left.'

It made sense in a way and gave them all something to think about – except for those who considered it an impossibility and not worth thinking about. Like Hondo and Howie Rainey. The others said little or nothing.

Half an hour later, Reno was showing the general some of the repeating rifles he had brought for him when Lucky came up carrying a bundle of women's clothing. It looked like elegant dresses and there was a hat with a large black feather in the band around the crown. She stood to one side until they noticed her and then looked at Martinez.

'You said this Vega has a blonde mistress, General?'

'*Sí*, a *rubia. Norteamericana.* She is supposed to be a lady from New Orleans. He is very jealous of her and it is said he fought a

109

duel with the sabres and killed one of his officers by cutting him to pieces because he had shown the *rubia* more attention than he should.'

'A jealous man – perhaps we can use that,' she said thoughtfully. 'But is he so infatuated with this Madonna that he would not look at another woman? One, say, showing a good deal of – bosom and with a – bold eye?' She was hesitant and Reno saw the flush on her cheeks and smiled to himself.

Then as she indicated the clothes she held he realized what she was saying. 'Now wait up! Don't you go getting any loco notions about going into that place dressed like some fancy whore...'

'Why not? You think I can't play the role?'

'Christ, I dunno, but what I'm saying is I don't want you to *try!*'

'Well, it's one way of getting across that drawbridge and into the prison area. I would need an escort of course, to come in with me, three or four armed men. Perhaps I could have a small troop waiting outside as well ... an "escort" through bandit country or something. It's a way to get in, Reno.'

'It's a way to get you killed, damnit!'

'The señorita with the so beautiful *rojizo* hair has a point, Reno, my friend – a very good point! I know Vega. His tongue would lick his belt buckle once he laid his piggy eyes on Lucky.'

'Forget it, General!' Reno snapped. 'She's not doing it.'

'There are a few uniforms in that cave as well as a variety of good women's clothing,' Lucky pointed out quietly. 'We could dress up some of the men...'

'These peons?' scoffed Hondo. 'It'd take a week of Sunday to scrub the dirt off them and get rid of the lice!'

'Have you ever seen *rurales* looking like store dummies, Hondo?' she asked sharply. 'No one looks past the uniforms. You could have twenty men waiting at the other end of the drawbridge with me and Reno and Howie and a couple of others already inside.'

'What about the rest of the men?' asked Howie Rainey. 'We'd need more if we aim to take over the prison.'

'They could slide down ropes over the cliff at the rear and be waiting for our signal...' allowed Reno. 'We've done that before during the War.'

He bit off the words, knowing now he was losing. The damn girl had a good head on her shoulders! Despite himself he was seeing the possibilities of it ... but he had remained quiet too long.

'Not losing your touch are you, Reno?' she asked quietly. 'Red told me about some of the hair-raising stunts you thought up during the War, in the midst of the enemy, too. And how nine times out of ten you pulled them off.'

'I didn't have you to worry about then,' he said bitterly.

She smiled. 'Well, thank you for your concern, but you did say you believed I could take care of myself – and I think I've proved that on several occasions...'

He sighed. 'Lucky, you've never gone up against a monster like this Vega. Chris'sake, woman, if anything went wrong, you'd face a death you wouldn't wish on your worst enemy.'

'If I'm willing to take that chance, what objections could you have?'

He shook his head slowly, looked around at the others and was surprised to find that while he might have the backing of Hondo, he couldn't be sure about the rest. They were looking thoughtful, uncomfortable maybe, but thoughtful – actually considering the girl's ideas...

She looked at him steadily. 'I think it's time we called a vote, don't you, Reno? Red said that was how you always settled something like this.'

Well, damn Red, he thought. Damn Lucky, too!

But he had been pushed into a corner and he knew he had to agree.

'OK,' he growled. 'Let's put it to the vote.'

Only Hondo, Howie Rainey and Reno himself were against – and, actually, Reno was wavering. It was audacious, her rough outline of the plan, but it could be refined and maybe with a lot of luck...

The majority was carried and a beaming smile from Lucky Cornell dazzled them all.

'OK, let's get down to the fine details,' Reno said with resignation, but his mind was already racing with workable ideas.

CHAPTER 8

THE TEST

They needed more uniforms.

There were maybe a dozen in the slop chest kept in the cave with other loot but the majority of them had either bullet holes or machete cuts mangling the cloth which was also heavily stained with blood. True, the womenfolk could wash and repair them up to a point, but Howie Rainey had said he saw a big, constant flash of light from the main watch tower of *Luna Roja* when he was there, observing, and he was sure it was a telescope with a large objective lens.

'Not that the *rurales* are what you might call stylish. That mustard brown makes my belly heave – but if they went calling on the Governor, like we're s'posed to be doin', or close enough for him to watch them through a telescope they'd need to be tolerably neat.'

'Why don't we ambush some of the Government cavalry?' asked Earl Handy. 'They got fancy rags, gold braid and all, and big hats to hide your face.'

'Can't Earl,' Reno told him. 'They're under control of the Governor and he'd know where each troop is supposed to be so they couldn't turn up as escort for unexpected guests without raising a heap of suspicion.'

'So where do we get uniforms of any kind?' demanded Craig Enderby.

'There's a small *rurales* post at Laguna Bustilos, out of the way but near *bandido* country,' Reno. 'It's more a relay station for their network of telegraph lines than a serious fighting unit according to the general, but there's up to thirty men there and an army store.'

Hondo King looked around at the ragtag peons as they lounged around the camp. 'We goin' up again that many experienced soldiers with this lot?'

'They fight OK,' Howie Rainey told him quietly.

'Yeah, but unless I miss my guess we gotta wipe out these here *rurales,* that right, Clint?' Hondo asked.

'Hondo's right – we have to wipe them all out, can't leave anyone behind who might get word to Vega.'

'All they'd have to do is send a telegraph,' put in Cole Gannon.

'Not if we wreck the line,' said Enderby, but Reno shook his head.

'Not too soon. That telegraph's gonna come in mighty handy.' He turned and looked towards the silent Lucky Cornell who was sitting on the edge of the circle, not contributing anything to the meeting as yet 'You told me you know how to operate a telegraph key, Lucky, am I right?'

She glanced at him sharply, then nodded. 'Red taught me one time – I can do it but I'm not expert.'

'You're the expert here – Red was our telegraph man during the War.'

She frowned slightly. 'You'll – want me along then on this raid?'

'Hell yeah. With or without the telegraph we're gonna make this a test for all of us. We're all OK in training and in theory. Now it's time to see how good we are in practice – hone the edges you might say. Anyway, the more *rurales* we wipe out the less trouble for us after Red Moon.'

The *Renegades* grinned at each other: it would be good to work side by side again in a real fighting situation.

Only the girl seemed more than a little worried.

It was a good excuse for General Martinez and his men to find some action, too.

The plan was for them to strike the village at Cuauhtemoc, pronounced *Quat-a-moc* and named after a long-dead Aztec chief who earned the ire of the early *conquistadors* and was put to death by torture. During the raid, General Martinez and his men, Howie Rainey included, would hit the village and sweep up a few women and some food and whatever they could loot. Reno and his men would isolate a telegraph pole for their use

116

to the north and at the general's signal – a simple series of dots-and-dashes – Lucky Cornell would connect their portable telegraph key to the wires and send an urgent message to the post at Laguna Bustilo that would bring the *rurales* a-running. Martinez's men would either ambush them – depending on how many there were – or lead them on a wild and fruitless chase back into the hills where, once again, they would either kill the soldiers or make sure they were lost for some days.

After the message was sent and acknowledged, Earl Handy and Cole Gannon would rip down the wires – just in case the officer at the post decided to check that there had indeed been a raid on Cuauhtemoc.

Then after the majority of the troops had left the post at the Lake, Reno would lead his *renegades* in, shoot up the place with lots of noise and yelling and generally take over. If they had to kill the remaining men then so be it, but it was imperative they gain possession of the telegraph station.

It was late afternoon when Reno brought his team into position.

They had ridden in from the north-west and the Laguna was in plain view. It was a small body of water, bean-shaped, with scraggy chaparral and a few *cacto* plants around the edges. Between the lake and the huddled village of Cuauhtemoc there was rocky ground, riddled with eroded gulches and two places deep enough to be called small canyons.

The long ragged line of telegraph poles snaked through this sun-baked country, some of the poles sagging drunkenly as the blasting hot winds blew away the earth that supported their bases. When they sagged far enough the poles' weight pulled the copper wires free of the insulators and sometimes snapped them.

This time, when it was right, they would have a little help.

Reno deployed his men, and the girl, along the ridge, choosing a place where they would get the increasing shade of the rocks as the sun sank lower through the golden haze of afternoon.

He glanced up at the sun and figured they ought to be hearing something from Martinez mighty soon. They had agreed to time it so that the raid on the village was made close to sundown – but not too close or the lazy *rurales* would not want to start out until the next morning.

Reno set his field-glasses on the buildings of the post at the southern end of the lake. There was little activity, but there were two raised guard towers, one at each end, and he knew the guards would be told to be extra alert after word came in about the raid on Cuauhtemoc. Well, it was going to be Cole Gannon's job to take care of those sentries, him being the best shot.

There were gates with sharpened stakes at the front and loopholes cut in them. There used to be a lot of Indian trouble up here at one time and the post had been there for years. In recent times there had been little action up here so he was hoping the men stationed there would be lazy and not too well trained.

At the same time, as this was to be a test for his men, he didn't want it to be a pushover: he wanted them to have to work at winning, for Red Moon would be no easy task to take and after all this time the Renegades needed experience.

He glanced towards the girl who was keeping herself a little away from the others. She was very quiet, spoke only when she was spoken to, but a couple of times she hadn't answered at such times and he figured she was deep in thought about – something.

'I think I heard what might've been gun-fire,' Craig Enderby called down from where Reno had stationed him high up on a needle rock. He had field-glasses to his eyes as he lay prone. 'Yep – there goes the general!'

'Damned if I'd like to be in that village,' allowed Handy. 'Those cut-throats will go plumb loco, wouldn't surprise me none.'

Earl Handy was right.

Of course, the general made no attempt to control them. They had been growing restless and some of them had been surly and disrespectful to him, earning lashes from his shot-loaded whip or a slash from his sabre. But he knew they needed action and this was just the kind that would keep them happy – women to rape and houses to plunder, livestock for fresh food, more clothes and trinkets for their camp women.

Around sixty souls lived in Cuauhtemoc and mostly it was a quiet life, rural in the extreme way out here, the constant battle with nature taking most of their energies. Anything they had had been hard won – and so they fought hard to hold on to their few possessions, harder than the general or his battle-hardened cut-throats had expected.

But the resistance put an edge on things

and after a ragged volley cut down three of the *revolucionarios,* two fatally, they threw caution – and mercy, if they had ever had an ounce of it in their systems – to the four winds.

They rode in shooting at everything that moved, whether it was in skirts or children's clothing or trousers. They swung blood-smeared machetes indiscriminately, burned the houses, shot terrified cows and pigs on the spot, later to be gathered and taken back to the mountain hideaway.

The women and young girls screamed as their clothes were ripped from them and they were flung to the ground or on the crude beds, anywhere they could be raped and, eventually killed.

The sun went down blood-red in colour and it was appropriate...

'Time to move down to the telegraph line,' Reno said, a mite reserved now that he realized just what he had unleashed on the innocent people of Cuauhtemoc.

Lucky Cornell gathered her gear without speaking and began to make her way down the rocky slopes with Reno and Hondo King. They stopped at a sagging pole and King climbed it agilely, taking the long wire with the clip that the girl gave him and followed her instructions as to where to attach it to the copper encircling the glass insulator.

She had a pair of headphones on and shushed Reno a couple of times when he was asking if she heard anything and then suddenly she smiled – faintly – and nodded, lifting one earphone.

'That's the signal – four dots, five dashes, followed by three dots.'

She had set up the small board with portable brass telegraph key on it, screwed down a couple of red-and-green coated wires to terminals and then grasped the knob on the brass arm and began to tap out her call for help to the post at Lake Bustilo, using its call-sign.

She made it jumbled but clear enough to be understood – giving the impression that it was sent in a hurry and under frightening conditions.

It went something like this:

Empleado! Empleado! Send help! Attack on village – many dead – muy sanguinario. We need help – they come–

She broke off in mid-word. The mixture of English and Spanish would add to the confusion. Even if the post *commandante* did not savvy much English he would get the message.

It was barely twenty minutes later when a mounted troop rode out, uniforms obviously hastily thrown on, visored caps riding precariously, sabres and their metal sheaths rattling and clinking, dirty white bandoliers across the chests of the flustered men. They were led by a slim man in a neat uniform and Reno figured he was the *teniente*.

They rode through that blood-red sundown with the lieutenant screaming urgent orders, urging them on with the flat of his sabre smacking across the sweaty rumps of the galloping horses.

'Seems to've worked,' Hondo King said and at Reno's nod took the heavy pliers the man handed up to him, pulled on thick leather gloves and cut through the copper wire. It *pinged!* and lashed free just missing his face, twanging as it coiled through the air and hung listlessly down the side of the canted pole.

'If they try to get through and realize a wire must be down,' the girl said slowly, 'will they send out someone to check?'

'Not tonight,' Reno said indicating the sun, most of its disc obscured by the hills now. Deep shadow crawled across the land.

Lights were appearing down at the post.

Reno looked at her carefully in the dimming light and said, 'Time to go down and get the uniforms.'

Her teeth flashed at him in a quick smile that he felt was somewhat forced and she said, *'Bueno!'*

He nodded and whistled softly like a gambel quail homing in on its nesting young ones, bringing them food. He listened and heard what might have been – but wasn't – the call of a Muscovy duck winging in to the lake.

They met up with the other *Renegades* down by a clump of needle boulders, formed up without any orders and turned and headed in towards the distant post which was closing down for the night.

Or forever.

The guard in the tower by the front gate – no more than a raised platform really, with a rail around the top – never knew what hit him.

He was silhouetted against the afterglow, rifle leaning uselessly against the rail, leaning on his forearms, smoking a cheroot or cigarillo. *When the cat's away* ... thought Reno, who signed to Cole Gannon to go ahead and get rid of the lazy guard.

Gannon slid his Indian flatbow from its deerskin case-and-quiver-rig combined, took out a metal-tipped arrow with five curving eagle feathers of fletching to stabilize the flight and make sure the missile travelled in as flat a trajectory as possible. He pressed the braided string deep into the nock and drew in one smooth movement as he lifted the osagewood bow, pushing with his left hand, pulling with his right, the fletching touching his face just beneath the right eye. It had hardly come into line before he released and the string twanged and there was a *whoosh!* and the guard grunted as the shaft buried itself to the fletching in his chest, just forward of his left arm, angling deep and destroying heart and lungs. The man slumped and slid back on to the platform with a dull thud.

The guard at the rear fared no better.

When Reno saw his shadowy fall through the glasses, he nodded to Earl Handy and Craig Enderby. They moved in on the heavy front gates. Reno had seen earlier that when closed with the inside bar dropped into place, there was still a gap of several inches between the edges of the gates. This meant there was several inches of the bar exposed and it required little effort to dislodge it.

Handy and Enderby slipped a rope around it first and Enderby held this as Earl got a forked stick into the gap and under the bottom edge of the bar. He strained to lift it high enough to clear the socket attached to the inside of the gate on the left hand side. He sweated some and grunted a couple of times but managed to raise the bar clear and he thrust inwards as the bar fell. Enderby took the weight on the rope and let it slide through his hands, swearing as it burned his palms, easing it silently to the ground.

The gates swung open a couple of feet and stopped on their stiff hinges, long un-oiled. On Reno's signal the men eased through, Lucky last. Her face was very white in the dim light.

'First action?' Reno asked quietly, but she only threw him a look that could have stripped wall paint and pushed past him into the post.

The men were moving fast, knowing just what to do, a little rusty, maybe, but unhesitating. Except the girl. She seemed lost and jumped when Reno grabbed her arm.

'Come with me. We've got to get that telegraph operator.'

Gannon led the men to the barracks

where there was some singing and laughter, and through a dirty window pane they saw about ten soldiers lounging on beds, three gathered around an upturned box between two beds playing cards. A tequila bottle was being passed around freely. Clearly those left behind were aiming to make the most of the *commandante's* absence.

Gannon glanced at the others and nodded and then kicked open the door and they ran in, spreading out, rifles braced into hips, firing into the men. It took the soldiers by surprise and four went down immediately, only one for certain able to crawl beneath the beds and snatch a heavy pistol from a dangling rig. He rolled on to his back, grimy undershirt stained with blood near his left shoulder, cocked the big gun and fired.

It boomed like a cannon and Hondo King's left leg kicked out from under him, depositing him in a heap on his side. He rolled off the wounded leg and triggered his rifle across his body, lever and trigger working rapidly. The man with the pistol didn't get another shot off. Hondo swore and ripped off his neckerchief, wrapping it tightly around his leg and the wound which was only a shallow groove in the flesh. Gannon threw himself headlong as one of the men at the far end of the barracks ran for a rack of rifles along a wall. He wrenched one free, working the bolt action on the Mauser and fired before it was in line with Gannon. The bullet ricocheted wickedly from the stone floor, sending men ducking for cover. Gannon shot the soldier between the eyes.

Two more men reached guns and turned, fighting. They might be lazy but they were long on guts, and aimed to go down fighting. Which they did. Handy and Enderby cut them down where they stood and the only Mexican left dived out the swinging rear door into the night. Cole Gannon was first through the door and drew his sixgun and fired all in one swift, easy motion.

The Mexican was punched several feet forwards and grunted twice before his face skidded on to the parade ground and he rolled into a rag-doll heap, unmoving.

Gannon started running for the other building, where the officers' quarters were and likely the telegraph room. A man in undershirt, with one suspender over his shoulder, bootless, started shooting with his heavy calibre pistol. Gannon dropped and rolled and came up on to one knee, fanned two fast shots that blasted the man back against the wall. As he slid down, there came gunfire from inside the building.

Reno led the girl into the smaller building and a man, looking sleepy, his uniform jacket hanging open, stumbled out of a room, groping awkwardly for his holstered gun.

'Knife!' hissed Reno but the girl only stared at him.

He swore and shot the man as he got the gun free. 'I didn't want to alert the telegraph man that we were this close, damnit!' he snarled as he thrust her aside and ran down a small passage to where he could hear a telegraph key clattering.

The lines running south to Red Moon were down but Gannon had warned Reno that the telegraphist might still be able to send a message north to the big army post at Chihuahua City once he realized he couldn't reach *Luna Roja*.

He burst into the room and the man was hunched over the clattering key, a gun in his hand pointed at the door. The gun was shaking, the barrel circling wildly, but Reno didn't hesitate. He shot the man twice and he fell with a clatter on to the floor. As Reno stepped forward he heard the girl gasp behind him.

'My God, that was nothing but cold-blooded murder! He wasn't going to shoot!

He was too afraid!'

He looked at her, face tight, eyes drilling into her.

'It shouldn't have been necessary. Tell me something, Lucky: you're fast with a gun, can shoot the eye out of a gnat at twenty paces, can throw that knife in your boot quicker than I can blink and you talk mighty tough about taking men's eyes out or cutting off their manhood.'

She glared back at him, nostrils flared, eyes wide, lips pulled tight across her small white teeth, bosom heaving with rapid, deep breaths.

'You sound like a walking killer, full of confidence – until it comes to the doing.' He reached her in two steps, grabbed her shoulders and glared down into her face, shaking her. 'But you're a goddamn phoney, ain't you? You've never shot at a man who could shoot back in your life – and you sure as hell ain't ever killed anyone, with knife or bullet! You're all goddamn – *talk!*'

He shook her angrily, her head lolling on her shoulders, and, just as Gannon came bursting in, she broke down and began to cry.

'I'm sorry! I'm so – sorry! I – I just can't do it. Red taught me how to kill but I – I've never shot at anything more than a target!'

Reno released her and looked at Gannon.

'Playtime!' said the gunfighter. 'That's all this has been for her – goddamn playtime!'

CHAPTER 9

READY TO RIDE

They dynamited the post at Laguna Bustilo, blowing up the storehouse and the barracks with its dead men, and, in particular, the telegraph building.

But before they demolished this latter building, Hondo King rode out to where they had broken the telegraph wire earlier and repaired the break.

They had found the communication books and call signs in a scarred drawer of a desk in the telegraph room and studied these before sending a message to *Luna Roja*. It was addressed to Governor Vega personally, prefixed with two words. *Importante!! Significante!* and the special call-sign of the Chihuahua Headquarters.

Prepare for visit Miss Lucinda Cornell – Chairwoman American Prisoners Welfare League. Riding with aides and escort of Rurales from Laguna Bustilo. Make welcome. Give freedom of Red Moon at your discretion. Diplomacy essential. Request direct from El President.

Lucky sent it smoothly and competently. Then they waited, knowing the authenticity would be checked by Vega. The query came fairly quickly, asking for confirmation and contained a code word that they had to look up in the communications book. It was merely to show that the request came from Vega's office. Lucky replied in the Chihuahua *commandante's* name rather tersely as would be expected from an officer whose orders were queried.

After Vega's hastily acknowledged acceptance and a request for arrival times – which was ignored – they destroyed the telegraph building and tore down the wire from several poles, north and south of Laguna Bustilo.

Then they dynamited the entire place and rode back to the general's camp where he and his men were celebrating their victory at Cuauhtemoc.

While the celebrations continued and

rurales' uniforms sere distributed and tried on, Reno took the subdued Lucky Cornell to one side.

'You're going through with this,' he said flatly. 'You might've figured it was fun coming up with ideas and hoping maybe we'd reject them or consider them too dangerous, but now we're past the point of no return. You're gonna have to brush off your acting skills and become Miss Lucinda Cornell of the American Prisoners Welfare League or whatever the hell we called it.'

She looked at him soberly. 'Don't worry, I'll go through with it.' Then her face softened a little. 'I'm sorry about what happened.'

'You could've gotten yourself killed. Or someone else,' he said a mite shortly. 'Baptism of fire is always a big deal. Best thing to do is talk to someone who can guide you through it.'

She nodded, although he had been expecting her to blow up. 'I'm ashamed, I didn't think it would be like that. I simply – froze... Red and I were very close, you know. We shared everything, even feelings. If I had a bellyache, he suffered pains or a stomach upset, too. If he was worried about something I could sense it and we would talk things out, exchange thoughts and

133

opinions. Red knew sooner or later he was going to meet a man faster with a gun than he was. So he taught me all he knew about firearms and defending myself.

'He said it would give me confidence. He hoped I'd never have to use it, but it was the only way he could think of so I could take care of myself when he was no longer around.'

Her voice was taking on a shaky sound and she paused, cleared her throat, brushed at her eyes.

'I thought it might be some kind of – memorial – to Red if I took his place in your team. Clint, I tried to measure up but it was all an act, and when it came to the pinch – well.' She spread her hands helplessly.

'Lucky, you have all the skills. Red did a damn good job. What you have to try and remember is that Vega's men are the enemy. If you don't kill them, they'll kill you. It's kill or be killed.'

'I can't see this as a war like you do. To me it's no more than a murder mission to kill this man in Red Moon prison – this Zachary Peglar.'

'That's what it is and if it takes a small war to reach him, then that's OK, too.'

'I just let myself get in too deep and now I

134

have to make it up to you, but – I – don't know just how well I can really carry out the impersonation.'

'It was your idea. We're stuck with it now.'

'Yes – I always could come up with good ideas. I see the solution to a problem and I just have to speak up. Clint, I know how important this is to you and I can't let Red down. So don't worry – I'll do my part.'

'Howie and me'll be close by but we still have to use you to smuggle in our guns. They won't dare search you.'

She was pale now but she nodded. 'Yes. I'll even wear my boots beneath all those skirts and with a knife in the top of each one. Just in case.'

He looked at her steadily and then smiled and surprised her – and himself – by lightly kissing her on the cheek.

The trouble was, now he was going to have to give half his attention to her safety in a situation that would need his full concentration if he was going to have any hope at all of pulling it off.

Red moon prison was a huge sandstone and granite oblong, high walls, raised guard towers, built on two levels like a step down. The lower level at the rear was where the main cells were, where the tortures took place – and the screams were muffled. The drawbridge spanned a wide chasm and was lowered upon their arrival, a chain winch clattering.

There was no problem in getting in. In fact, the 'official party', comprising Lucky Cornell in her finery from the *revolucionarios'* slop chest, Reno dressed in frock coat and flowered vest, and Howie Rainey, dressed in similar fashion, with Miguel Boca, looking neat enough in reasonably clean, if worn, traditional Mexican clothes, were welcomed enthusiastically. It made Reno suspicious right away.

The 'escort' of twenty *rurales*, as expected, were not admitted to the prison. They were halted at the far end of the drawbridge and an officer of the *Luna Roja* showed them where to camp some distance away, out on the naked plain. They were not to approach closer than ten yards to the end of the drawbridge, should call to one of the wall guards and explain their business if they did. Otherwise they would be shot.

He spoke to them like the rabble he assumed they were, not knowing that General Martinez himself was dressed as one of the rank and file. When the officer had gone back into the prison, Martinez spat.

'Mark that one well!' he hissed. 'He will be one of the first to die!'

In the hills that rose behind the big fortress-like prison *Reno's Renegades* were making their way to the top, carrying their gear, keeping out of sight. The prison was built so close to the cliff face that it would be mighty difficult for anyone down below to see movement up on the top unless it was at the very edge.

Governor Vega was a large man, not unduly tall, but he cut a fine figure in his dusky green uniform. His skin was dark but glowed with a health and vitality known in the prison section of the fortress. He wore medals and ribbons on his thick chest, and a black leather belt and harness, with a large English Webley pistol in a polished holster at his side. His face was round, the eyes restless and dark, the lips purplish, bracketed by a curving black moustache. His teeth were very white. He was not an unhandsome man and he knew all the courtesies and dusted them off when he welcomed Miss Lucinda Cornell and party.

His dark eyes sparkled for the woman when he bent over her hand and kissed it lingeringly, but they were flat and suspicious

137

as he regarded Reno and Rainey. He totally ignored Miguel although Lucky introduced him as her interpreter, adding with a smile, 'My Spanish is far from faultless, your excellency.'

It would do no harm to have Vega believe they knew little Spanish.

'My English also,' he smiled back, saying *Eengleesh*. 'We will take refreshments and you can tell me what is the purpose of your visit to *Luna Roja*.'

Lucky frowned a little. 'Why, that's simple, excellency. You have at least one American prisoner here and it is the function of our League to travel wherever a fellow American is incarcerated and to make sure he has all he needs.'

'Ah, your League, then, is an official Government department?'

'We operate with a Government grant so I suppose you could say, yes.' Reno admired her quick answer.

Vega merely nodded. 'The *Americanos* have tried many ways to break down my resolve not to release Señor Zachary Peglar into their custody – I can not seem to make them understand that the man was involved in an assassination attempt on *El Presidente* and therefore he is a political prisoner. He was most fortunate not to have been condemned to death.'

'Was that, perhaps, excellency,' Reno said quietly, 'so Peglar could be used as a political pawn if it became necessary…?'

'You are being undiplomatic, *señor*,' Vega cut in curtly.

'When may we see this Peglar, Governor?' asked Lucky, frowning at Reno then immediately dazzling the Mexican with a smile.

He offered her his arm which she took – not having a choice – and said, 'Later perhaps – maybe tomorrow. I believe it is not convenient for him to receive visitors today.'

She arched her eyebrows as he led the way across the carpet to large double doors where uniformed servants waited to usher them into the reception he had prepared.

'A prisoner says it's not "convenient"? Surely that is unusual, excellency!' Her query held just the right amount of incredulity and Reno saw that Vega did not like it.

'*Señorita*. You must understand we have a different prison system here. If a man can pay his way, he may arrange for his own apartment and food and – pleasures.' There was something bitter about the way he

139

spoke the last word and Reno became alert, catching the swift flash of frost in the man's eyes. 'It is condoned by Mexico City and such a person, of course, is entitled to some consideration. We use the money for the benefit of all prisoners, naturally.'

'Sure,' whispered Rainey as he and Reno brought up the rear behind Vega and Lucky. 'Get a new bull whip, or a pair of pincers or a set of chains.'

Reno smiled thinly and shook his head briefly, warning Rainey to keep such thoughts to himself. Vega glanced over his shoulder but his expression was unreadable.

'It is my information that Señor Peglar is ... entertaining privately this afternoon. I could, of course, put a stop to that but if I did, you would wish to leave by sundown. This other way, I will be able to offer you my hospitality overnight.'

Lucky paused, looking sidelong at Reno. 'I – I'm afraid we won't be able to avail ourselves of your kind offer, excellency. We have a schedule and–'

'Nonsense,' he smiled, taking a firmer grip on her arm and urging her into the large hall where the table was laid out with food and drink. Uniformed officers stood around at attention. There were some women at the head, one tall and stunning with golden hair.

Reno figured this was Vega's favourite, Madonna.

'You must stay overnight, *señorita*. I insist, and I am sure your League and Government would not wish to offend me – an official representative of Mexico...?'

'Of course not, excellency, it's just that we have limited funds and if we don't keep to our schedule we–'

He laughed. 'But your stay here will cost you nothing. It is settled.' He snapped his fingers and two uniformed officers hurried across. He spoke rapidly in Spanish and Reno and Rainey were led away through another, smaller door. Boca was escorted down the passage.

'You will forgive the necessity,' the tall officer said when they entered a dim room with only one window. The officer snapped his fingers.

Out of the shadows stepped four men two holding rifles across their chests, hard-eyed. The other two gave each of the *gringos* a thorough body search. They found no weapons of course. The officer smiled ingratiatingly even executed a small bow.

'Your forgiveness, *señors,* but it is necessary. Our Governor is a most important person.'

'Forget it, *teniente*,' said Reno pleasantly enough. 'We don't carry arms. Where has our interpreter been taken?'

'He will eat in the kitchen. Now, we return to the reception.' The lieutenant unsmiling, escorted them back to the big hall where Lucky, looking flushed, was laughing at something Vega had said. The man was leaning towards her, holding an overflowing glass of brandy in one hand. It was obvious he was entranced by her beauty.

The Madonna of the golden hair was looking at Lucky with knives in her stare.

'If that *rubia* don't have green eyes, she damn well ought to,' murmured Rainey.

Reno was seated along the table from the Governor and Lucky Cornell. 'We've got to figure some way to get word to Cole and the boys that Vega's got us nicely tied-up here.'

But there was no chance of that. The reception went well, with entertainment by guitar, singers and dancers. Vega seemed to be laughing louder and more frequently now, had an arm across the back of Lucky's chair. She looked nervous while Madonna seemed positively murderous.

The lieutenant came and leaned down

142

between Reno and Howie Rainey at the table. He said quietly, 'It is time for me to inspect the night guard, *señores*. Per'aps you would care to see some of our – amenities...?'

It left them little choice and Reno glanced down the table at Lucky and saw the concern on her face as he and Rainey stood and followed the lieutenant out of the room.

The man took them towards the rear of the building and down some stone steps to rows of cells. None were lit and the escort seemed to make sure their hand-held lanterns did not illuminate the smelly cells beyond the first few feet. They heard moans and once a pitiful plea for mercy but they did not actually see any of the prisoners – except for the dirty, battered feet of one protruding from the shadows. There were no nails on the torn and bleeding toes...

Reno and Howie exchanged a glance. *Why the hell were they being shown this...?*

The answer came soon enough. They were shown into a vacant cell and the lieutenant said,

'This is a typical upper-level cell. Roomy as you see.' Then, with a quick, well-rehearsed shuffle he and the armed guard were outside with the door closed and locked in seconds.

Reno rushed to the small barred window in the door. 'Hey. *Teniente,* what the hell're you doing?'

The lieutenant and his men were moving away down the passage. He called back without looking around. 'Do not worry, *señor,* all is well. It is the Governor's little surprise. He thinks it good that people who concern themselves with the welfare of prisoners should experience some of the conditions for themselves. It is a fine idea, eh? *Buenas noches, señores!'*

No amount of yelling did any good and the Americans soon gave up, groped about in the pitch blackness and found a bunk each. They were here for the night. *At least...*

'Son of a bitch!' said Rainey feelingly. 'The whole deal is one big trap!'

'Yeah – Vega's a lot smarter than we gave him credit for! You know what he's done, of course – he's not only separated us, but now has Lucky as a hostage.'

CHAPTER 10

RED MOON

'But where are my friends?' Lucky asked the drunken Governor Vega as he and some guards escorted her along a dimly-lit passage to a room at one end. She sounded – and was – very concerned.

Vega waved a hand airily. 'Do not concern yourself with your friends, *querida*. They are well accommodated. Ah! Here is your room. I have had it specially prepared for you.'

It was a very feminine room, all lace and gold and deep reds and contrasting pearl greys. A large double bed with several pillows, ornate bedside tables and chairs, heavy drapes on the walls arranged artistically against the bare stone that had been smoothed over. It was a room of cold charm. Very nice for an overnight stay but one that Lucky wouldn't wish to have to return to night after night.

'It's lovely, Governor, but – I am worried about my friends. And my interpreter.'

145

He smiled slyly, squeezing her arm intimately as he leaned towards her and spoke huskily, eyes lively. The brandy on his breath was almost overpowering. 'I think your Spanish is *excelente!*' He waved a finger in front of her face, laughing. 'And you try to be modest and tell me it is not very good.'

'Your English is near perfect, too, *señor*,' she told him. 'Yet you said you do not speak good English!'

He laughed again, spreading his arms. 'I must plead guilty, *señorita!* But then everyone has some leetle thing to hide, eh?' He lifted her hand and kissed it gently. 'I wish you *buenas noches, querida.* We will see each other in the morning.'

She only wanted rid of him and smiled and gave a little curtsy, feeling the weight of the two sixguns strapped to her thighs. They were heavy and had caused her to walk awkwardly. She would be glad to take them off.

Her heart was pounding as she went inside, after first refusing the services of a maid, and closed the door.

She would wait a while, then slip out and try to find Reno and Rainey.

But she was more tired than she reckoned and when she lay down on top of the bed covers she slept despite her resolve. And just as she started to wake up enough to remember she wanted to search for her friends, there was a rustling sound. In the dim light of the turned-down lantern she watched with widening eyes as one of the curtain drapes against the wall slid aside and Governor Vega stood there. He still wore his uniform but it was unbuttoned now and there was no side-arm.

He saw her sit up quickly on the bed and smiled as he came forward, carrying a decanter of wine and two glasses. He smiled. 'Ah, *bueno, querida*. You are expecting me, eh...? I say we see each other "in the morning" and now it is after midnight – I am a man of my word, *querida!*'

He quickly set down the bottle and glasses on a small white table with ornate gilded legs and rushed towards the bed with open arms.

'Ah! The delights that await us, *mi belleza!*'

She started to swing her legs off the edge of the bed but he was upon her too soon, his greater weight pressing her back, hands already pawing.

She tried to reach the knife in the top of her boot but he had one leg across hers, pinning the skirts. She struggled and felt his hands tearing at the cloth and gasped,

'Wait! Let me!'

He smiled crookedly as he eased back and she pulled up the skirts a little way and groped beneath.

'Ahhh! You like me, eh? My Madonna is already jealous, but–' He shrugged.

Suddenly her hand came out from beneath the voluminous skirt and he reared back, eyes and mouth wide, as the dim light reflected from metal. Without pausing to think, driven by fear, her heart pounding, Lucky swung the sixgun and crashed it across the side of the Governor's sweaty head. He grunted and stumbled to his knees, a hand going down to support his upper body as he swung his head dazedly, watching the small drops of blood falling beside his supporting hand. He raised his head, face slack, and she hit him again.

This time he collapsed, unconscious – and there was more blood oozing from a fresh gash.

Lucky, panting, sat back on the edge of the bed, looking down at him. Then she composed her face and fought to control her breathing. She had taken an inevitable step and now she had to get out of here. The passage door was locked on the outside –

but the Governor had entered by some sort of door behind the curtain.

She glanced at the man again, dropped the sixgun on the bed and pulled the drape aside – but a blank stone wall faced her. She peered closer, bringing the lamp over and turning up the wick. She could see the small gaps in the mortar marking the outline of a narrow door but there was no apparent handle.

She tried pressing every stone, pulling on the drapes' cord, then used her knife blade to try to prise the door edge open.

Nothing. She was locked in the room with the Governor – and soon he would begin moaning as he started to regain consciousness.

'Damn you, Reno! Where are you when I need you?'

She flung herself on the bed, mind racing, trying to find a way out of this mess.

Reno and Rainey had a visitor, too.

Reno was dreaming of a man with a twisted, scarred face, wearing an eye patch and, as he turned slightly he also saw the mangled left ear. He made a groaning sound and then felt heat on his face and smelled hot oil – and he knew he wasn't dreaming at all.

There was someone beside his cell bunk

leaning over him, holding a lantern close: Zachary Peglar.

Reno sat up so fast he struck his forehead against the metal base of the lamp and Peglar smiled, stepping back, brining up his other hand and showing Reno the short wooden club he held.

'Well, you ain't changed much in ten years, you son of a bitch!' The club moved a few inches, hard and swift. It cracked across the lower part of Reno's face, opening the flesh. He grunted and fell back.

There was a scuffle behind him and a thud and when his eyes came back into focus he saw a Mexican with a rifle standing over the prone, unmoving figure of Howie Rainey.

Peglar laughed, a wet, throaty wound. 'Don't worry, he ain't dead – yet. I'm savin' you both for somethin' real special. Waited a long time, and, fact is, I never figured I'd get the chance, 'cause ol' Vega, corrupt as he is, don't aim to ever let me outta here. I can buy a club but not a gun – and I can get outta my room most anytime I want, but when my money runs out, I got real problems. But mebbe I'll have somethin' figured out by then...' He leaned closer as Reno dabbed at the blood on his face. 'That wife of yours was a real beauty, Clint. How come a killer like you finished up with somethin' like her – real sweetmeat, she was.'

Reno swung his legs up and as Peglar jumped back, slammed his boots into the man's face. Because he was going backwards at the time, the blow didn't have the force Reno would have liked, but it knocked Peglar halfway across the cell and put him down on one knee.

Then one of the two armed Mexicans he had entered the cell with stepped forward and slammed his rifle butt against Reno's head. He fell back, spiralling down into a dark pit shot through with spinning lights.

Peglar got groggily to his feet, nose and mouth bleeding. As soon as he saw the blood on his groping hand, he swore, stepped forward, dragged Reno from his bunk and began kicking the unconscious man until one of the guards dragged him off. Peglar rounded on him but the other covered him with his rifle. Reluctantly, Zachary Peglar lifted his hands waist-high, fingers spread.

'No trouble – I'm OK now. I got in a couple of licks. How about I try for a couple more?'

'I think your visit is finished, *señor*,' said the man who had pulled him off Reno. 'The Governor has his own plans for these two. I

151

do not think you will be disappointed in their fate.'

'Ah! I got a woman waitin', anyway. To hell with this scum!'

Peglar spat on Reno and took one more scathing look around before storming out into the passage. The guards followed, one pausing to lock the door.

Lying prone at the edge of the cliff that rose so vertically from behind Red Moon prison, Cole Gannon lowered the field-glasses. He had been studying the upper part of the fortress, where the Governor had his living quarters and where the sounds of *fiesta* came faintly to him. The lenses were not gathering enough light to show him much but he could watch the lighted windows here and there.

'Any sign yet?' asked Hondo King coming up beside Gannon, kneeling on one knee.

'Nary a thing. That party seems to be windin' down. But no signal at all.'

'Sure we would've seen it?'

'Reckon so – they were gonna hold a lantern to a mirror to reflect the light. It would flash brightly and we'd be able to pick it out easily enough. They could be in trouble.'

'What I was thinkin'. Somethin' must've gone wrong.'

Gannon rolled on to this side, looking back to where Craig Enderby and Earl Handy waited. 'You fellers game?' He asked quietly.

'Say the word!' growled Handy. 'That damn gal's the trouble. Din' come up to scratch at Bustilo. Too good-lookin'. A damn bull like Vega would've had her earmarked and set up soon as he set eyes on her. I reckon she's the problem.'

Gannon swore: he hadn't thought of that kind of trouble but–

'Mebbe we better give it a little longer.'

'Hell, man,' Enderby said, 'the ropes and grapnels are ready. So're we – we could be down the cliff and over the back wall in half an hour!'

Gannon hesitated – he was in charge of this part of the operation. 'No, we wait. Clint won't make a move until he's sure everythin's goin' to work. Give it another hour and then hell or high water we go in.'

In the early hours of the morning, Reno and Rainey woke out of their rifle-butt-induced sleep to hear the door rattling and then screeching as it dragged across the stone floor when it was opened.

Reno rose groggily on his elbows and saw figures moving against lamplight in the passage. They flung a limp, unconscious form into the cell and the door slammed shut quickly, the key turning in the lock.

'Some company, *señores!*' a man said, chuckling, through the barred window.

'Christ! Who is it?' Rainey slurred and Reno slid awkwardly off the bunk and crawled across.

He fumbled out a vesta and struck it on the stone floor. There was a huddled, ragged and bloody form lying just inside the doorway. The man smelled of sour vomit and burned rags and singed flesh.

'Whoever it is has been tortured, I'd say. Covered in blood. No finger or toenails and seems to be a helluva lot of cuts … aw, hell, it's Miguel!'

Rainey came off his bunk as the match went out and Reno struck another. It was Boca, all right, barely recognizable, and they now gently turned him on to his back. He groaned.

There was a small stone bowl of water in one corner and they washed his swollen and battered face and he rolled his head side to side and slowly came round.

'Miguel – it's Clint and Howie. What the hell happened to you?'

He was a long time responding and then

154

only in grating monosyllables. The story was brief, and deadly. One of the *revolucionarios* who had been taken prisoner weeks earlier was his oldest son. Vega's men had used this lever on him and got word to him that if he betrayed General Martinez's group his son would be spared the firing squad. Miguel had finally weakened, sent word to Vega about the plan to break in and kill Peglar – which was why Vega was ready and waiting for them.

They took him away when Reno and Rainey were locked in this cell, but not to show him where to eat. They made him watch while they hung his son from a wooden beam, saying, 'See? We keep our word – no firing squad!'

He went berserk and so they beat him and amused themselves by torturing him and then threw him in here to die along with the *gringos*.

'I'm sorry for my – be-trayal… It was not – honourable…'

'You did what you had to, Miguel,' Reno told him quietly. 'Vega will die for this – and a lot of other things. You've got my word.'

Miguel clawed at him with his broken hands, mouth working, trying to say something, but the effort was too much for him and he slumped back, gagging, the death rattle croaking in his throat.

Reno sat back on his heels and sighed. 'Well, poor Boca won't give 'em any more amusement. At least we know what went wrong.'

'Sure – but we're still in here with no way out!'

They were stretched out on their bunks, smoking, not much later, when they heard voices out in the passage.

Reno went to the small barred window and looked out into the dimly lit passage. He saw the back of the guard who had been outside the door walking away from the cell. He had to flatten his face hard against the door and look sidelong to see down the passage.

'Hell! It's Vega! I can just see part of his uniform past the guard.'

Rainey came over beside him. 'Judas, I hope the others didn't get tired of waitin'!'

'They were told only to act on the signal. No signal, no action... Christ! Vega's got Lucky with him! She's holding his arm!'

Rainey swore. 'I hope what I'm thinkin' ain't what's happenin'!'

'The guard's coming back and Vega and the girl are following...'

Reno stepped back from the door as a key rasped in the lock and it swung open, revealing the guard. He had propped his rifle against the wall, but started to pick it up as he turned towards Governor Vega and the girl.

'She looks different,' Reno thought to himself and quickly realized what it was – she was wearing her narrow-brimmed riding hat and a checked shirt above the waist, but the voluminous skirts below. Then things began to happen.

The Governor seemed to lunge at the startled guard who dropped his rifle with a clatter and clawed at his master to keep from falling. Both men stumbled through the doorway and went down in a tangle. The girl stood with a cocked six gun in her hand, looking inside anxiously.

'Reno? Howie?'

They moved quickly, hauling Vega off the struggling guard, flinging the big Mexican aside. Reno kicked the guard under the jaw and knelt swiftly, unbuckling the man's revolver belt and holster. He buckled the rig about his waist quickly as Howie Rainey snatched up the guard's rifle, worked the lever to open the breech and saw that it was fully loaded.

Both men stared at the girl who was busy

shedding her skirts. She wore her riding breeches beneath tucked into the top of her high buckskin half boots.

'He came to my room and tried to force himself on me,' she said as she shed the skirts, handing Reno the sixgun she had held on Vega. 'I knocked him out with that gun but couldn't find a way out. So I waited until he came round and held my knife against his crotch. I didn't say a word. He just sweated a lot and told me in a very small boy's voice that he would do exactly as I said – anything at all!' She gave them a quick smile. 'So I said take me to my friends, and here we are.'

Reno smiled thinly, taking his own Colt and handing Rainey the Mexican's pistol. It was large and of European make, probably French. Howie rammed it into his belt.

'You're doing good, Lucky! We've got to get a signal to Gannon.'

'I already have. The only window in the room faced the rear and the cliff, so while I was waiting for Vega to come round I held the lantern to a mirror and flashed the sequence to come in. They should be coming over the rear wall by now.'

'Well, we have to coordinate and somehow get the drawbridge down for Martinez.'

He was turning to the governor who had

now discovered Boca's tortured body and was hurriedly moving away, when there was a shot and a shout from along the passage.

'The relief guard!' yelled Rainey working the rifle and shooting back. A bullet screamed off the stone walls of the passage and the girl gave a small cry as she ducked, produced the second Colt she had smuggled in and fired. She gave a gasp as the guard up there at the passage entrance spun away wildly and fell to one knee. Rainey finished him with a rifle shot and then they were running away from the cell as more guards appeared and the rifles fired with ear-shattering cracks in the confined space. Bullets ricocheted with vicious snarls.

Reno dropped to one knee, twisting so that he faced the guards at the far end. He fanned the six gun, figuring the hail of bullets would scatter them, not worrying about finding any particular target. One guard fell and didn't move. A second snatched at his shoulder and the other two dived for cover.

By then, the trio were around the corner of the passage and they stopped dead at the sound of a dull explosion from the prison section beyond the building where they were.

'That should be Gannon blowing the prison gates,' Reno said as the girl handed

159

him a box of ammunition she took from the pocket of her trousers.

He grinned his thanks and nodded his approval of her thoughtfulness and broke open the box, thumbing fresh loads into his gun.

They heard the heavy boots of guards coming down the passageway and he and Rainey stepped out, guns blazing. Rainey braced the Mauser rifle against his hip, working trigger and bolt action, the slower pace punctuating the crash of Reno's six gun with hammer-blow sounds.

Some of the guards were only half-dressed, obviously having been routed out of their beds. They heard Vega's screeching voice but didn't see him as he bawled frantic orders.

The guards went down in a tangle and those still on their feet began to run back away from where Reno and Rainey waited. The two men, having stopped pursuit for the time being, went back around the corner in time to see Lucky shoot a man who stepped out of the shadows with a shotgun. He went down hard, dropping the gun, trying to crawl towards it.

Rainey finished him and the white-faced Lucky gave him a sharp look and then Reno grabbed her arm and pulled her with him as they ran down a wide hallway towards what he figured was the front of the building.

They heard shooting and shouts vaguely from the prison section, some screaming, and another dull explosion. Reno slowed, thinking they had better see what was happening with Gannon and his men and then Cole Gannon and Earl Handy appeared, dishevelled, covered in rock dust from their wild slide down the ropes at the cliff face and the climb over the rear wall.

Gannon was carrying his bow and arrow and he had two arrows with something tied to the end a few inches above the metal barbed tip. Reno recognized sticks of dynamite with short fuses.

'Get to the drawbridge!' Reno shouted and Gannon nodded – clearly that was his destination, anyway. Handy held back.

'You folks OK?'

'Now – thanks to Lucky,' Reno answered and he saw what he thought was gratitude and pleasure in the girl's face ... but only for a moment.

They came to an arched doorway that led to the short tunnel beyond which was the drawbridge and its lowering mechanism.

There was a chain locking the winch handle to the stone floor but Gannon was already kneeling, a dynamite arrow fitted to his bow, snapping a vesta into flame to light the fuse. Three armed guards ran out of the shadows, shooting and Reno and Rainey – and the girl – fired back, bringing down all three.

By then Gannon had shot his first arrow and even while it was in flight he had notched the second and was lighting the fuse. The first arrow smacked into the wood of the raised drawbridge at the upper right-hand corner. Reno ducked, twisting away as it exploded and blew a section of wood and holding chain free. The second arrow drove home at the opposite upper corner and blasted out the section on that side that held the holding chain and its heavy plate. The twisted metal clattered loudly on the stone walk and then, there was a snapping of chains as the heavy bridge, freed of constraint, tilted forward by the dynamite blasts and crashed down across the chasm, raising a cloud of dust and shaking loose rocks and debris that clattered and thudded down into the dark depths.

Beyond, in the half-light, they saw Martinez and his bunched 'rurales' waiting. He lifted a hand and the riders started towards the lowered bridge, shouting and yelling wild cries.

The thunder of the hoofs drumming on the bridge almost drowned out Reno as he said to the others,

'Now – let's go find where they're holding this son of a bitch Peglar!'

CHAPTER 11

MOONSET

Martinez and his men were ruthless. Anyone wearing the uniform of the governor's soldiers – or even part of it – was shot where they stood or run down with the horses, some of the fired-up Mexicans wheeling their mounts and spurring back over the prone and broken bodies several times.

They swept through the governor's living section and charged across the parade ground and courtyard to the rear gate which led down to the prison. These gates had been blown off their hinges by Gannon's men, as had the heavy wooden gates leading into the prison.

Inside there was a complete riot. Craig Enderby, Hondo and Earl Handy had released some of the prisoners, but not all of them were Martinez's *revolucionarios*. There were others who had managed to survive the torture chambers and had not yet had to face the firing squads and the scarred wall.

There was blood everywhere and the men had armed themselves with machetes and tools from the worksheds. When Martinez and his riders appeared, he shot down some of the prisoners along with any surviving guards who actually ran to him, screaming for mercy.

'Free your comrades!' he shouted, throwing down on a running guard while a prisoner chased him with a machete. 'Free the liberty fighters! Kill anyone else who gets in the way!'

His men were only too willing to do so and already there were several fires burning. Men who had suffered in the torture rooms had strapped some of their tormentors on to the benches and to the poles and swung others from dangling, bloodstained chains. Then they spilled oil all over the satanic machines whose only purpose was to inflict pain, and also some over the screaming men.

They locked the doors behind them on the way out as the first flames took hold...

Already the first streaks of a red and gold dawn were writhing across the sky. Some of the dark swirling smoke rose amongst them, carrying the screams of the doomed with it.

In the west the moon was almost down, fading from red to amber in the layer of dust that perpetually lifted from the treeless plain.

'I heard Vega order a guard to check the "apartments" before they put me in that room,' Lucky Cornell volunteered as she followed Howie Rainey and Reno down the long passages. 'The guard went along the passage that crosses this one – I think he turned right but I can't be certain because I was worried about what was going to happen and Vega wouldn't tell me where you and Howie were.'

'OK,' Reno said, taking her elbow and nodding at Rainey. 'We've got nothing to lose. Let's go right, Howie.'

They went to the cross passage with guns drawn and Reno instinctively pushed the girl behind him as they rounded the corner, hammers back, Colts ready.

And just as well.

There were four guards in full uniform with rifles and pistols waiting about five yards along the intersecting passage, blocking it completely. They began firing as soon as the trio appeared.

Reno triggered with one hand, and pushed Lucky flat with the other. Howie dived headlong towards the guards, gun thrust out ahead, firing swiftly. One of the guards grabbed at his throat, rifle clattering to the stone floor, staggered into another, knocking his gun aside. Bullets scarred the flagstones and ricocheted from the walls. Reno triggered and his hammer fell on an empty chamber.

He rolled on to his side, fumbling in his pocket for loose cartridges and reloading awkwardly.

'Reno!' the girl cried and began to toss him her pistol, but suddenly renewed her grip, turned and fired at one of the guards who was kneeling and drawing bead on Reno. Her bullet took the man in the face and smashed him flat.

Reno reached up, snatched the smoking gun from her hand and pulled her down.

He twisted and triggered again, taking one of the two remaining guards in the chest. A second later Rainey's slug finished the other man.

Reno helped the girl up, offering her the pistol again. 'Good shot,' he said, looking steadily into her pale, worried face.

'I – just instinctively fired. I didn't mean to–'

'You're a dead shot,' he told her harshly. 'You saved my neck. Thanks – now let's find Peglar before they slip him away.'

Rainey was already relieving the guards of their pistols, ramming two into his belt and reloading his own Colt awkwardly. Reno replaced his used shells and they went on down the dimly lit passage, trying doors cautiously.

One room obviously belonged to a woman, the air heavy with perfume. Dresses and other feminine clothing were scattered about untidily. Lucky pointed to the pale green frock with the low-cut bodice draped carelessly over the end of the huge bed.

'Madonna was wearing that at the table.'

Reno nodded: this was Vega's mistress's room but there was no sign of the woman. *Too bad, he thought. They might have been able to use her as a hostage...*

There was a narrow door with elaborately-carved erotic images connecting to another room. Obviously this belonged to Governor Vega, but once again there was no occupant. They searched swiftly to make sure and Rainey shook his head.

'He'll be wantin' to save a payin' customer. Wouldn't surprise me none if there was a secret escape tunnel somewhere.'

'All we can do is keep looking,' Reno said with resignation and they went out into the long, twisting passage once again.

After passing through two turns, they came to a section where there were three doors set widely apart. The first one was unlocked and they looked into a darkened room. Rainey fetched a wall lantern from the passage and they found that they were in one of the 'apartments' – set up as a sitting room, with separate bedroom. It wasn't actually a bed, but it was wider than a bunk and there was only one in the room which had clothes closets and small tables and chairs for relaxation. Prisoner's heaven in miniature.

The window looked out over the jail section and to the edge of the cliff, beyond which part of the plain was visible.

'Room with a view,' commented Rainey.

But it smelled dusty and didn't look as if it had been used for some time.

'Next one,' Reno snapped, hurrying now.

He was almost level with the second door when he heard a muted scream from behind the third door, followed by a man's shout and then a fusillade of heavy gunfire.

The trio sprinted along the passage towards the door, guns ready.

Reno stood to one side, Colt cocked in one hand, the other holding the spare gun Rainey had taken from one of the guards they had shot. Howie turned the handle but the door was locked.

'To hell with it!' Rainey gritted and shot the lock out with two bullets, following swiftly with a driving kick that slammed the heavy door back against the wall with a crash.

Reno leapt past him, crouching, both guns ready to fire. He stopped dead in his tracks.

Zachary Peglar lay face-down on the floor, two bleeding bullet holes in his back, one hand stretched out close to the wooden club he had used on Reno earlier.

There was a monotonous moaning sound and Reno flicked his gaze up.

In a chair across the room sat Governor Vega, with the naked body of Madonna clasped against his chest. Her arms hung limply and her golden hair had been released from the comb that had held it earlier, spilling down over her shoulders. Blood dripped slowly from a part of her body that was against Vega, soaking his uniform. He was stroking the long hair tenderly with one

169

hand, his face wet with tears.

Lucky stepped up beside Reno as Rainey closed the door and leaned against it, face hard and without expression as he looked at the distraught Vega.

'Killed 'em both. Jealous, yet he tried to rape Lucky.'

'Some men think there are two sets of standards,' she said curtly and Reno looked at her quickly. She met and held his gaze.

Vega looked up now and slowly recognition came into his eyes. 'She knew I would not stand for her being with a prisoner, in apartment or cell. She was jealous of Señorita Lucky from the start.'

'With cause!' snapped Lucky. 'You planned to rape me all along!'

'I thought you cared for me.'

'I was being polite! That's all! You damn pig!'

His eyes narrowed and he moved his gaze first to Rainey and then to Reno.

'What now? You have taken Red Moon?'

'Not quite – now it's time for settling a few debts. For all the men you've had tortured and put to death over the years – including Miguel Boca and his son.'

Vega's expression didn't change and he continue stroking Madonna's hair.

'My way is all the filth understand or expect – but it was also my job. What will you do, kill me?' He shrugged and went on before Reno could answer. 'It doesn't matter now that I have lost my Madonna.' He paused and spat on Peglar's corpse. 'He thought his money could buy anything – but he will not need *dinero* to enter hell!'

While speaking he slid his hand between the woman's body and his. Suddenly he sent her tumbling to the floor. He snarled, bringing up his big pistol, hammer back.

Reno fired once with both weapons, the Mexican pistol making a thunderous crash and almost leaping from his hand with recoil. Vega's gun triggered as the impact slammed him out of the chair, the bullet ricocheting briefly.

He died with a loud snoring sound. Lucky's face was tight and pale, but there was no expression on it as she watched Vega's final twitches.

'So Vega beat us to it,' Rainey said with a gritty sound as he came forward and used his boot to nudge Peglar over on to his back. He grunted and doubled over, pressing a hand into his side.

'God-*damn!*'

He staggered, wincing.

171

'You hit?' asked Reno moving towards Rainey.

The girl was already at his side and tried to support him as he went down on one knee. Reno knelt beside him, prised his bloody hand away from his body.

'That ricocheting bullet tore a chunk outta you, *amigo*. Wouldn't surprise me if it's busted a rib.'

'Nor me,' Rainey gasped, wincing. 'Think it might be – two...'

The girl helped Reno get him to the bed in other room.

'I can patch his wound and bind his torso with the sheet and cord from the drapes if you'll lend a hand.'

'Let's get it done.'

It took a good ten minutes. Reno left once or twice to go to the door with the broken lock and check the passage. He could still hear sounds of battle in the prison section, but there was no immediate menace from outside.

'All clear so far.'

Rainey was pale and dazed, but luckily the bullet had gone right through, only cracking the ribs on its way. Lucky supported Rainey on one side.

'We'd better be going, hadn't we?'

Reno glanced back at Peglar.

The eyepatch had come loose and the wrinkled, sunken socket stared up at them from the ugly, scarred face. Light caught the convolutions of the mangled ear. Reno suddenly reached down and startled Lucky when he pulled the knife from the top of her right boot. The blade flashed.

He loosened the eyepatch and put it in his pocket, looked over his shoulder and said to her, 'Wait outside with Howie.'

'What're you going to do?' she demanded.

'Just wait outside, damnit!'

The wounded Rainey started to move and she either had to go with him or release her hold and allow him to fall. She went with him, reluctantly, pausing to look back through the partly-open door.

Reno was kneeling beside Peglar, knife in his right hand while he reached for the man's mangled ear with his left.

She closed the door quickly.

Outside, the day was coming fast now, spreading across the desolate plain and the smoking ruins of Luna Roja. Ragged men, grimy with blood and gunsmoke, were gathering outside the walls with many skittish horses. Some were already mounted.

In the west, there was the faintest hint of rosy glow where the red moon had finally set.

CHAPTER 12

THE COLONEL

Martinez was sad and emotional when it came time for Reno's *Renegades* to leave.

He had been drinking of course, to celebrate the victory, and maybe that accounted for the dampness in his reddened eyes as he gave each member a crushing hug. He gave Reno two, leaving the man gasping for breath.

'You are still my *gringo extraordinario, amigo!* You will return some time?'

'Could be, General. You've got a lot more men to help you in your struggle now. When they make you *El Presidente* you send for me and I'll come.'

Martinez laughed, but there was sadness in it.

As they prepared to leave, Howie Rainey said, 'Reckon I'll come back to the good old

US with you, Clint.'

Lucky, cinching up nearby, turned sharply. 'What about Dolores? And the baby?'

Rainey shrugged. 'Dolores is about as exclusive as a drinkin' pail.' He shook his head emphatically. 'I ain't takin' the responsibility.'

'Of course you're not!' she said bitterly, eyes blazing. She flickered her angry gaze to Reno. 'And I suppose you back him up?'

'It's Howie's decision. But when I was here before, Dolores sure did play musical bedrolls.'

'Oh, you damn men!' She started to turn away, spun back, almost shaking with her anger. 'You know, I don't think I'll ever have any more trouble if I have to shoot a man – in fact, it'll be a pleasure!'

She mounted and spurred away from the camp, giving a casual wave by way of farewell. Reno watched her go, frowning slightly. He hadn't wanted it to end this way...

'Who can ever savvy women, eh?' Rainey said, wincing at a stab of pain from his side.

'I think Dolores does favour you, Howie.'

'Mebbe. But I'm goin' back home, Clint, and that's that.'

Reno let it go. This was Rainey's way and always had been. Then he said, 'Just be sure to send her something out of the bonus the colonel's paying us.'

It sounded like an order and Rainey's eyes narrowed a little before he said, 'Sure – I'll do that.'

Reno wasn't sure he meant it.

He looked around at the others, preparing for the long trail back.

Gannon was sitting on a log cleaning his guns, unscathed, restless, likely impatient to get back and look for another fight somewhere.

Hondo was smoking a cigarillo, leaning an elbow on a bent knee, thoughtfully watching a young *señorita* in swirling skirts as she danced for a group of cheering, half-drunk men.

Earl Handy was favouring his wounded hand with the missing finger. He looked longfaced, jaw on his chest. He had tried manipulating a pack of cards but had spilled them everywhere. His gambling prospects did not look good.

Reno's gaze moved to a bundle of clothes with a hat resting on top of a folded gunrig beside them. They had belonged to Craig Enderby who hadn't made it out alive. Well, he had been alive when they found him outside a cell block with a deep machete slash across his chest and another that had

176

almost severed his right arm. Alive enough to make Reno promise that he would see that his wife received all the money that was due and to tell her that he died doing the thing he liked best – fighting alongside his brothers-in-arms.

That was one chore Reno sure wasn't looking forward to.

At the Border, they scattered to the four winds, a brief handshake, a rough joke to cover any emotion that might try to slip through their guard.

'Try trainin' your pecker to slip a card from the bottom of the deck, Earl!'

'Hey, Cole – be safer if you found a woman to sleep with instead of that rifle you're always cuddlin' up to!'

'So long, Howie – you better learn to treat women decent before you wake up some mornin' with somethin' important missin' from under your belly!'

'Hondo – you're gettin' old now. Know what they say: use it or lose it!'

Reno sat atop Cherokee Butte for a long time, watching their various dust trails thin out and finally disappear under the hot Texas sun.

He wondered if he would ever see any of

them again.

'You didn't do the job you were hired for!'

Colonel Skinner scowled across his desk, glaring at Reno who stood before him, trail-stained and weary. Stretch Kincaid lounged against a wall, arms folded, watching Reno closely.

'He's dead, damnit!' Reno said tightly and dropped a small, cloth-wrapped bundle on the desk top.

The colonel glared. 'What's this?'

'What you asked for.'

Skinner picked up a round ruler and poked at the cloth, opening a fold or two. He wrinkled his nose when he saw the reddish-brown stain of dried blood, snapped his cold gaze at the silent Reno, then barked at Kincaid: 'Come and open this!'

Kincaid frowned, didn't move right away, apparently not liking being ordered about like some sort of slave in Reno's presence. Then he thrust off the wall with his wide shoulders and walked slowly across to the desk, pulling his gloves tighter before beginning to unwrap the cloth.

He held up a wrinkled black eyepatch on a thin rawhide string, and dropped it in front of Skinner. There was a thick brown paper square lying in the middle of the cloth, stained and ugly-looking.

Kincaid peeled back the layers of paper, grunted, and then thrust the object across beside the eyepatch. It was Peglar's mangled left ear.

'Get that filthy thing out of here!' roared the colonel thrusting to his feet, face dark with anger.

For a moment, Reno thought the tall gunman was going to refuse. But he gathered up the wrappings and the eyepatch and ear and took them out of the room. Reno leaned his hands on the edge of the desk, boring his gaze into Skinner.

'Peglar's dead. You owe us four thousand dollars each for the balance of the fee – I've an idea it's not much use asking for the bonus you mentioned.'

'You're right there. And wrong elsewhere.'

Reno tensed. 'The hell does that mean? Seven of us did the job, so that makes $28,000 you have to cough up.'

Skinner's thick shoulders hunched as he leaned forward. 'Neither you nor any of your *Renegades* killed Peglar. Vega shot him.'

There was a dangerous tightening of Reno's wolfish features but the colonel chose to ignore it – or didn't deign to even notice.

'We went down there to kill Peglar – or to make sure he was dead. Craig Enderby was killed. Three were wounded. Lucky Cornell, Red Rogan's sister, was almost raped.'

'She had no right to be there. Once you learned Rogan was dead, you should've replaced him with a man.'

Reno was surprised at how quickly he sprang to Lucky's defence. Kincaid returned at that moment but Reno didn't move his gaze from the colonel.

'She's an excellent shot and can throw a knife even better than the Mexicans. She rode into battle with us and saved my life!'

Skinner shook his head. 'You shouldn't've taken her. She's not eligible for any money.'

'You damn piker! She risked her neck right along with the rest of us.'

'Another thing, this Enderby who was killed – he certainly wouldn't qualify. What the hell use is money to a dead man?'

'You gave your word that the family of any man killed would be paid whatever was owed to them.' He glanced towards Kincaid now. 'Kincaid heard you.'

Skinner glared at his gunfighter intimidatingly. 'Did you?'

'I believe what you said was you'd give it your "consideration".'

Skinner smiled crookedly. 'Well, I've considered and as the entire mission seems to have been accomplished by someone else, my decision is that I'm not obliged to pay anyone.'

'You go along with that?' Reno asked Kincaid tautly.

'I work for the colonel.'

'Can you sleep nights?'

Kincaid set bleak eyes on Reno but said nothing.

The colonel seemed amused. 'I'll reimburse you your expenses – can't be fairer than that.'

'Try.'

Skinner's face coloured. 'Do I hear a threat somewhere there?'

'Right on top.'

'By God, don't you try to shake me down in my own house, you son of a bitch! Kincaid – throw him out!'

Kincaid started forward and Reno turned to meet him. The gunfighter was fast, looked loose-limbed, but there was nothing loose about the blow that skidded along the side of Reno's jaw, snapped his head back hard enough for his hat to fly off. Reno spun and Kincaid was on him, hammering at his kidneys and spine, grunting as he drove home each blow.

'Mind the furniture, goddammit!' bellowed Skinner.

Kincaid moved around, fists cocked as Reno's legs buckled. He threw two straight lefts into the man's face, hooked with a right which Reno somehow managed to dodge. Then Reno charged with arms spread wide, wrapped them around Kincaid's wiry frame, pinning the gunfighter's arms to his side.

The momentum carried them across the office and they struck the balcony doors at full speed. Wood splintered and glass shattered as they crashed through on to the balcony itself, rolling about, broken shards of glass crunching beneath their scrabbling boots.

They staggered upright together, both cut and bleeding. Reno got his hands up to protect his face as Kincaid came round swinging. The blow almost broke through Reno's guard, but he deflected it, ducked under the man's arm and slammed a maiming tattoo into his midriff. Kincaid back-pedalled and his legs wobbled as he ducked and weaved.

He caught one of Reno's fists in his gloved hand, twisted and brought the man stumbling in close. With his free hand he drove three up-swinging punches into Reno's ribs. Reno grunted and writhed in pain and it drove him wild so that he roared and stepped back in suddenly. The move threw Kincaid out of his rhythm and he staggered to one side. It gave Reno room to swing and hook the gunfighter in the rib cage, at the same time butting his head into the man's face.

Kincaid lurched back with blood streaming from his nose and mouth, his jaw feeling like it had been kicked by a Missouri mule on a bad day. He shook his head in an attempt to clear it and the slight pause was all that Reno needed.

He crouched, hands up, weaving, looking for an opening, and when he found one he stabbed a straight left against Kincaid's already bloody nose. The man howled, wheeled away, and as he came round to face him again, Reno hit him on the jaw with a looping right that sent Kincaid lumbering backwards until his legs hit the rail. He grabbed so as to keep balance and he was wide open for the uppercut that lifted him to his toes. As he started to fall, Reno cut loose with a wild tattoo that drove the gunfighter down all the way.

He lay huddled, breathing hard with bubbling sounds, unable to get up.

Skinner spun and rushed back into his study. Reno stumbled after him, wanting only to sit down somewhere and soak his aching hands in ice water – and to pour a gallon of the same down his burning throat. He slipped on the broken wood of the door frame and more glass crunched under his boots as he grabbed the upright for support.

By the time he had pulled himself up straight and stepped into the room, Skinner had a pistol out of his desk drawer and he cocked the hammer and coldly drew bead on Reno.

'Far enough! Don't think I won't shoot!'

Reno stopped, too weary and breathless and disgusted to make any reply. He leaned his weight on his right hand in the doorway, head hanging as he settled his breathing and spat some blood on to the carpet

Skinner flushed. 'You bastard! Oh, I really don't know what Elanor was thinking about when she married you!'

'Told you once – she was desperate to get away and seemed I was the only man she'd met who offered to take her out of this damn house!' He paused and added a mite viciously, 'She jumped at the chance.'

'Liar! She loved me! You talked her around, filled her head with lies. She didn't know what she was doing!'

'She knew. Told me once she'd forgotten what real freedom was like, that she'd never been happier.'

'Oh, you'd like me to believe that, wouldn't you?'

'I don't give a damn what you believe. Elanor's dead and now she's been avenged. You put a price on that and now you'll pay up.'

'It'll be a cold day in hell when I let you tell me what to do, Reno!'

'Better put on your fur jacket, then, Colonel, because today's the day.'

Skinner blinked and then laughed. Harsh and brief. 'Today's the day you die, Reno! To hell with you and your mercenary scum. You all should have been shot after the War for what you did to the Union. Well, it's been a long time coming, but I'm about to redress that oversight. *Adios,* Reno!'

The gun lifted one inch and Reno drove down for his Colt, having to push off the doorframe first, slowing his draw.

Colonel Skinner screamed, loud enough to be heard even above the sound of the gunshot, and snatched at his blood-spurting right hand as the bullet tore through flesh and tendons. The gun bounced across the desk, fell off on to the floor, and fired once into a cupboard.

Reno spun, his Colt still clearing leather. He froze as he saw the blood-streaked Kincaid standing behind him, smoking sixgun in hand.

'What the hell? You aim at me and miss?'

'I hit what I aimed at – most always do,' Kincaid said as he stepped into the room. He jerked his gun barrel at Reno's Colt. 'You want to holster that?'

Reno hesitated, frowning at the man's tone and the look on his bloody face. Then he leathered his unfired gun. 'You'd never have beaten him – his hammer was falling before your gun was clear.'

'Then you're no damn slouch!'

Kincaid shrugged. 'I could shade you easy – but we don't need to get into that. He's got enough money in his safe to pay what he owes you. I know the combination.'

Stretch Kincaid walked forward, pushed the moaning, sick-looking colonel down into his desk chair and tore off Skinner's silk neckerchief from around the fat neck. He bound the shattered hand, bringing cries of pain and bitter curses to Skinner's lips.

Reno, mopping blood from his face with his own neckerchief, hitched one leg across the corner of the desk. 'Why're you doing this?'

Kincaid looked at him. 'You ain't the first one he's welshed on. Figure it was only a matter of time before he pulled the same deal on me. Thing is, I wouldn't've minded goin' along on that Mexico thing. If I had've, he likely wouldn't've paid me, anyway. Just keep an eye on him – he's a tricky old bastard.'

'You're dead men! Both of you!' Colonel Skinner snorted. The pain had added a whine to his voice and a little sob between gulping breaths. 'You think I can't find someone to put you in Boot Hill...?'

'If they're smart, they'll ask for payment up front,' Reno said, watching as Kincaid moved a cupboard aside revealing a small but strong-looking safe set into the brick wall.

Kincaid leaned forward and began to play with the dial. Skinner watched tensely.

'How'd you get that combination!' he snapped as Kincaid finally swung the door open, revealing the shelves inside packed tightly with money.

'Once told you when you wanted me to do

some dangerous job that I never take chances, I like to know my escape route ahead of time and so on, have my getaway money stashed where I can pick it up fast. I just took a look around your desk a couple of times, when you weren't here, and eventually found a paper that had the safe combination on it ... how much you figure he owes you, Reno?'

'Twenty-eight thousand is what's due, but I think maybe another ten for all the trouble he's put me to.'

'Make it forty thousand, even,' Kincaid said easily. 'There's fifty thousand in here so I'll take the extra ten thousand as payment owed to me.'

'You goddamned thief! How the hell're you so generous with my money!'

'If you weren't such a skinflint, Colonel. How about that, huh? Not Colonel Skinner, but Colonel *Skinflint!*'

Reno smiled crookedly. 'Kinda like that...' Kincaid thrust the money into canvas bags taken from a shelf inside the safe and tossed the heaviest to Reno who caught it left handed. Kincaid smiled thinly.

'You got some good moves – and you're mighty careful.'

'Which is how come I'm still alive. Well,

thanks, Kincaid. One I owe you.'

Kincaid stood, holding his own bag of cash. 'Where you headed?'

'Couple of calls I've gotta make. Pay this money to the people who earned it.'

Kincaid arched his eyebrows. 'You really gonna do that, huh?'

'What'd you think I was gonna do with it?' Reno asked slowly, heavily. 'Keep it?'

'Crossed my mind.' Kincaid lifted a hand, palm out, hastily. 'No offence – I'm just beginnin' to see I been listenin' to old Skinflint here for too long. You gonna pay some money to the dead man's wife, this Enderby?'

'She's entitled.' There must have been something in Reno's voice.

Kincaid squinted at him. 'But…?'

'She hates my guts. She'll blame me for getting her husband killed – and she'll be right.'

'But – you're still gonna take her the money?'

'I just told you, she's entitled.'

Kincaid sighed and shook his head slightly. 'Think I remember bein' just like that once – long time ago, though. How about some company? Kind of a backstop?'

'You?' Reno was genuinely surprised.

Stretch shrugged. 'Nothin' for me here.'

He shook his bag of money. 'Don't have to work for a spell.'

Reno grinned. 'Why the hell not? Let's go.'

As they stepped through the broken doorway, the wounded colonel looked up and said, 'Wait – I've just had an idea. Men like you are too rare to let get away. Say we make it a business deal. I could find work for you both – for your *Renegades*, too, Clint! Make it a family affair, eh…?'

As they climbed over the balcony rail, Kincaid said, 'Don't give up easy, does he?'

Reno shook his head and they started for their horses. They could just hear the colonel's voice still calling, 'We could come to some arrangement – good percentages all round … I know I could find chores for you – written contracts this time if you like. What d'you say…?'

There was no reply.

He kept calling out suggestions, sounding more and more desperate, until, at last, he heard the clatter of hoofs fading into the distance.

'Then I'll have you hunted down and *killed!*' he choked in final desperation, shoulders slumping as he realized the bitter futility of the empty threat.

The publishers hope that this book has given you enjoyable reading. Large Print Books are especially designed to be as easy to see and hold as possible. If you wish a complete list of our books please ask at your local library or write directly to:

Dales Large Print Books
Magna House, Long Preston,
Skipton, North Yorkshire.
BD23 4ND

This Large Print Book, for people
who cannot read normal print,
is published under the auspices of

THE ULVERSCROFT FOUNDATION

... we hope you have enjoyed this book.
Please think for a moment about those
who have worse eyesight than you ...
and are unable to even read or enjoy
Large Print without great difficulty.

You can help them by sending a
donation, large or small, to:

**The Ulverscroft Foundation,
1, The Green, Bradgate Road,
Anstey, Leicestershire, LE7 7FU,
England.**
or request a copy of our brochure for
more details.

The Foundation will use all donations
to assist those people who are visually
impaired and need special attention
with medical research, diagnosis
and treatment.

Thank you very much for your help.